The Burning

Bride

GHOST HUNTERS SOCIETY

Book Three

Adria Waters

Printed in the United States of America
Copyright © 2017 by Adria Waters

Published by: H2O Press

ISBN-13: 978-0-9973424-9-9
ISBN-10: 0-9973424-9-8

This is a work of fiction. Names, characters, places, and incidents
either are the products of the author's imagination or are used
fictitiously. Any resemblance to actual persons, living or dead,
businesses, companies, events, or locales is entirely coincidental.

Cover by Covered Creatively

For Mom.
All my love.

CHAPTER 1

Breathe. One foot, then the other. She glanced up from her feet and smiled at her soon-to-be husband through her veil. *Breathe,* she reminded herself as she made her way up the soft grass aisle on the arm of her grandfather. His grip was strong, comforting, with a tinge of sadness. As she walked, the music floated around her in the garden. She looked over and nodded slightly to find the source of the music and saw a man playing a violin near the lilacs. The notes lilted along the breeze, carrying her on nervous legs to the gazebo at the front of the crowd.

Late spring was in full bloom in middle Missouri, and the gardens around the park exploded in a cacophony of bright colors. The fragrance was a mixture of the heavy perfume of peonies and the sharp sweetness of honeysuckle, vying for attention with the bouquet of roses she cradled in the crook of her left arm. She breathed deeply again and focused on not tripping over the hem of her flowing white dress. Her mother had spent days sewing it, lining the satin bodice with ivory beads that glinted in the early afternoon sun.

The bride peered up front, seeking her mother's gaze. She smiled. Her mother was there, dressed in a lovely mint green dress with a high lace neck. It was the last thing her father bought her mother before he died, and it had always been folded in a box in the attic of the house they shared with her grandmother and grandfather. A smile parted her mother's lips and she brought a gloved hand up to dab at her eyes with a handkerchief. The bride tried to send feelings of love to her mother. She wanted her to know how much she loved her, how indebted she would always be to her, but the veil shrouded her face and the best she could do was smile and move forward.

When they reached the end of the aisle, her grandfather took the end of her veil in his age-spotted hands. He pulled the veil out and up over the Juliet cap on her head and let it fall, the tulle floating on the breeze before coming to rest on her back. His foggy eyes regarded her for a moment and he leaned in close to her. He spoke, his breath soft upon her ear. "My sweet one, your father would have been so very proud of the young lady you grew up to be."

Tears burned her eyes and she blinked furiously, fighting for control over her emotions. "Thank you, Grandad," she managed around the lump in her throat.

He kissed her on the cheek. His wrinkled lips were like wisps of sandpaper against her skin. Then he took a step back and stood behind her as she handed her bouquet to her maid of honor.

"Who gives this bride to this groom in marriage?" the minister asked.

Her grandfather cleared his throat. "Her mother and I do."

Looking up, the bride met the deep brown eyes of her fiancé, James Miller. Her senior by ten years, he grew up in St. Louis, the only son of a wealthy family in the brewing industry. He attended St. Louis University before dropping out to serve during the Great War, but he never saw any fighting. His talent for the printed word suited him more for President Wilson's Creel Committee, writing pro-war propaganda. He came to Culvers Grove two years before in a sky-blue Moon Roadster that blew a tire on the outskirts of town. Her grandfather offered him a meal and a place to spend the night while his car was being repaired, and she fell head over heels for him the moment they met over a dinner of pork chops and baby red potatoes. Just like that, his plans to drive to California dissolved and he took a job with the local newspaper and asked the beautiful young woman to marry him.

She loved him so very much and he adored her, showering her with gifts bought with his father's bank account and ordering construction on a beautiful Victorian home on the outskirts of town. She fluttered her eyelashes at him and smiled. He was a good man. Though she tried to hide most of them, he never questioned the strange things that happened to her.

Since she was old enough to remember, she had seen people that weren't there. When she was little, she played with a small boy that lived in her grandparent's attic. He was so much fun, daring her to run full tilt at the stairs and leap over the space, landing in a pile of bedclothes on the other side. He loved to read, and she spent hours reading to him until the light of the day faded and she was called to dinner.

She presented her hand and watched as James slid the ring on her finger.

"This ring is my sacred gift to you. With this ring, I thee wed."

Once, and only once, she asked her grandmother about him. They were sitting around the modest table in the dining room, bowls of vegetable soup in front of them, steam wafting up into her nose, when she heard a thump from above.

"How come the little boy doesn't come down to eat with us?"

She remembered the sound of a spoon clanging into a bowl and the wide eyes of her grandmother.

"You, y-you are not to speak of him!" her grandmother shouted, pushing away from the table, a napkin held over her mouth as she disappeared into the kitchen.

The grandfather pushed his chair back and tossed his napkin on the table. He stood up, regarding the girl with kind eyes. "The little boy, the one upstairs," he glanced up at the ceiling, "what does he look like?"

The little girl was afraid to talk and looked to her mother for help. The mother nodded and the little girl spoke. "He is younger than I am, about four years old, and he wears a white shirt and gray pants." She paused and smiled. "He has brown hair and it's always wet."

Her grandfather's face paled and his hand trembled as he reached up to rub his chin. "You are no longer allowed to go into the attic. Do you understand?"

The little girl spoke, tears running down her cheeks. "Yes, sir."

When her grandfather left to comfort her grandmother, she turned to her mother, whose eyes were flooded with tears of her own.

"Why is Grandad so angry?"

Her mother gathered her in a hug. "My brother, William, drowned in a pond when he was four years old."

The words left her mouth as she slid the ring on James' finger. "With this ring, I thee wed."

She remembered sitting near the attic door, listening to the little boy cry. It went on for years, but faded. She never went back to the attic. The bride pushed the memory down and took a deep breath, trying to focus on the minister's words as they droned on. James held out his hands and she took them, glad to have something to lean on as her knees shook. *Breathe. Breathe. Don't get upset.* She closed her eyes and focused on the warmth of James' hands and the sounds of the afternoon.

"Found yourself a rich one, did you?"

Her eyes flew open and she stared over James' shoulder at her grandmother. The old woman's face was set, mean and judgmental, her gray eyes sizing the bride up as they had every day of her young life. She stood straighter, trying to show that she was in control, and that she was *fine.*

Her grandmother scoffed. "You're a fool and a good for nothing, just like your daddy was."

The words stung and the bride took another deep breath. *Leave me alone.*

"What are you going to do when he finds out?"

He won't.

"Oh, but, he will. And when he does, he'll leave you so quick it'll make your head spin." The old woman nodded her head, a nasty smile spreading on her face. "You can count on that."

The bride squeezed her eyes shut and counted to ten. When she opened them, her grandmother was gone. She focused on James and attempted a smile.

He furrowed his brow and stared at her.

Did he know? Did I say something out loud? Her mind spun, her palms sweating inside his hands that were suddenly too hot. She yanked them away and took a step back.

"Dear?" James said, his eyes kind. "Did you hear the man?"

She shook her head, panic gripping her as she realized she hadn't heard anything the minister said the last few minutes.

James chuckled. "Could you please repeat that last line? My sweet bride will want to hear it."

The minister cleared his throat. "You may seal your vows with a kiss."

Relief washed over her and she took a step forward, into the embrace of her new husband. She lifted onto her tiptoes to meet his tall frame and felt his arms wrap around her, and then his lips were on hers and everything was right with the world.

The wedding party followed the new couple down the aisle and received the guests as they left. The photographer took a picture of them as they were about to climb into James' car to leave for their house to change, before setting out for their honeymoon at Niagara Falls. He helped her into the car, carefully placing her skirt and veil on the seat before kissing her and closing the door. He had just taken his place behind the wheel and turned the key when his best man, Phillip, ran up to the car.

"James!"

He turned the car's engine off. "What is it?" He smiled, hanging an arm over the door.

"I have been called out of town on an emergency." Phillip spread his hands wide. "The factory can't run without me." James raised an eyebrow as Phillip handed him a piece of paper. "I know it's not usually done, and believe me, I would stay if I could, but I really need to leave."

James cocked an eyebrow and took the paper from him. "You want me to drop off the marriage license."

Phillip smiled, the corners of his eyes crinkling. "Thanks, man. You're the cat's pajamas."

James got out of the car and shook Phillip's hand. "We'll take care of it. Thank you for coming."

He strode around the car and opened the door for her, helping her out onto the curb. "My wife," he said, gently brushing a wisp of hair from her forehead, "would you accompany me to the City Hall to turn in our license?"

She smiled and took the arm he offered, content to wear the beautiful gown if but for a few more minutes. She found herself enjoying the stares of the people while they passed by along the sidewalk, as they walked arm in arm in the late April afternoon.

"The house will be finished by the time we return from our honeymoon," James said. "Mother is ordering furniture as we speak."

She placed her hand over the other that rested lightly on his arm. "I appreciate all that your family does for us, James."

Something passed over his face and was gone. The sun went behind a cloud and the colors of the day were instantly muted.

They came to the steps in front of the City Hall and walked up them, while she held the bottom of her dress up so she didn't trip over the long skirt. She stopped on the porch of the large building as James opened the door for her. A wind blew up from the yard, catching her veil and tossing it around her. The gossamer fabric floated in an ethereal halo around her head and in front of her face.

She squinted and thought she caught a glimpse of a man leaning against the brick façade of the building. Her veil came to rest around her shoulders and she blinked. No one was there.

She went through the door James held open for her. "Thank you, my love," she said as she passed through.

"I love you, my dearest Sarah," he said in reply.

The door banged shut behind them and the man on the porch pushed himself away from the brick wall. With hands shoved deep in his pockets, he counted the seconds until they would reappear and walk down the steps and along the sidewalk to the waiting car. That was his favorite part. Seven hundred twenty-three seconds. They would approach the desk and speak with the clerk who would take the paper from them and enter the license into the registry. They would stare at each other, the affection almost palpable between them, and he would remember when she used to look up at him with love in her eyes. When she was his. His little girl. They would steal a kiss and then emerge from the building, her cheeks pink with youth and excitement, his eyes full of the promise of a lifetime of happiness. Four hundred sixty-seven.

He adjusted his newsboy hat and brought his hands out of his pockets, the memory he played so often bringing a smile to his face. Two hundred forty-four. Almost there. He turned so that he could watch her come out of the doors like a million times before. Three. Two. One.

The doors came open and there she was. His sweetest memory. The most beautiful bride. He wiped at his eyes. The grandfather was right, he *was* proud of her. Every moment of every day. She swept past him, the scent of honeysuckle rising from her as she passed by.

He stood at the edge of the porch, watching, waiting for his favorite moment; the moment when his little girl turned and *saw* him. That moment when his life and death meant something. He could replay this memory over and over again and never get tired of it. He watched, not allowing himself to blink as she stopped in the yard of the courthouse, her white dress almost blinding as the sun came out from behind a cloud. His chest hurt, trying to contain the love he felt for her, his sweet baby Sarah. Oh, how he missed her.

She turned, her eyes searching, and then it happened.

In the memory, she locked eyes with him and recognition washed over her face. Confusion, a slight smile, and a hand raised to him in a slow wave. She *saw* him. He felt the dam burst forth in his chest and the emotion beat against his body from the inside out, hurting all over as he longed for this moment to never end.

He could exist forever in this moment.

As he watched, her image wavered. Something shifted in front of him, as if someone took a hand and wiped it over the memory. Just like that, it was changed somehow. He felt the change and shook his head. *No, this isn't right.* He tried to shift back to start the memory over again, but it was stuck, the afternoon frozen in time and space. The memory started and ended within this moment and he couldn't get back to the before. The wind shifted, bringing the scent of smoke with it. His nostrils flared and he coughed. It smelled wrong, like death.

He gazed down at his daughter, the breath catching in his throat. It took a moment for what he was seeing to register, but when it did, a roar escaped from his throat, tearing it raw as it wound its way from his core.

Sarah was burning.

She screamed, engulfed in a column of fire that blocked out everything in his line of vision. The silver-blue flames licked at her dress, turning it black, melting it onto her body, and burning the veil away. It floated on the air as it turned to ash.

"Sarah!" he cried. He tried to get to her, but was driven back again and again. She was on fire, screaming in agony and he couldn't get to her. Something inside of him broke as he was shown this new memory over and over again. It took over his entire consciousness until it was all he knew, all he had ever known, and all he would ever know.

"Make it stop! I can't take it anymore!" he cried.

Samuel, the voice hissed, *you know what to do to make it stop...*

CHAPTER 2

I sat up, rubbing the sleep from my eyes. Outside my window, the trees were covered in a thin layer of ice and the snow was already coming down. *No way would they have a snow day the first day back from winter break.* I rolled over and checked my phone anyway. When my suspicion was confirmed, I threw my phone back on the nightstand and dove into the cocoon of warmth under my paisley comforter, pulling the edge over my head. Everything about the day already felt wrong and I just wanted to go back to sleep.

Grant left for Kansas City two days before. I tried to tell myself that it wasn't going to be so different with him two and a half hours away. After all, we hadn't gotten to see each other much while he was commuting back and forth to Trenton and working every weekend. *Still...* Something about the move away felt permanent. When we said goodbye on New Years' Eve, he promised he would text and call all the time. I bit my bottom lip, already feeling like something was ending. When I left St. Louis almost three months ago, Piper promised the same thing. I pushed back the anger. She hadn't even called to wish me a Merry Christmas. *Things will be different with Grant.* Then, *will they?*

My door opened and feet scuffled across the rug. There was pressure as someone sat down on the end of my bed.

"Move your legs." Evie poked me in the thigh.

I moved my legs but didn't emerge from my cocoon.

"First day back at school," she said, her voice muffled.

I nodded.

"Excited?"

I shook my head.

"You haven't been out of the house since Grant left." Evie grabbed the edge of the cover and yanked it down. Static electricity bit at my hair. "Nice look, St. Louis."

"Shut up." I scooted up and rested my back against the headboard, my knees drawn up to my chest. The mention of Grant stung. He texted when he got into

Kansas City and sent pictures of the dorm room he shared with a guy from Troy. His name was Jeremy and he was a business major, too. Grant started classes Monday and said that they were going to be tough, but manageable. He ended his text with a ghost and a tiara emoji.

Evie tucked the end of the blanket over her legs. "What's wrong with you this morning, anyway?"

I sighed. *My boyfriend's gone. My mom's dead. My dad pays more attention to you than to me lately. Oh, and there's the little matter of something evil killing our friend, Sam, while I watched, and by the way, all the people we thought we helped are in more trouble than before we started. Any of those sound good to you?* I shook my head. "Nothing."

"You do remember that I can still see colors coming off people, right?" She narrowed her gaze at me.

"What do you see? Coming off me now?"

Evie tilted her head. "So, all around you, nearest your head and shoulders is a blue. It feels calm and full of love. It's actually quite nice."

"It's actually quite nice," I mimicked in a British voice.

Evie ignored me. "There are splinters of red and black coming out of that, though. They seem agitated and keep moving around. What are you thinking about?"

"Nothing, never mind." I threw the covers back and slid my feet into my ragged bunny slippers. Dad found the eye of one under the refrigerator and I'd reattached it with duct tape. That bunny resembled a deranged pirate now. "I have to get ready. So do you," I added, grabbing my towel from the back of my desk chair.

"What do you think today is going to be like?"

The uncertainty in her voice stopped me short and I turned, my hand on the doorknob of the bathroom. My best friend sat on my bed, her long, curly black hair piled on top of her head in a messy bun, and a T-shirt with a spaghetti stain over the faded Led Zeppelin logo. Dark circles clung to the bottoms of her eyes. She looked thin and tired and…well, *scared.*

I hung my towel on the doorknob and sat back down on the bed. "What are you worried about?"

"I'm scared about seeing everyone today at school."

I mulled that over. "It's a short week. You only have to be there three days before the weekend, right?" I went on. "So, everyone already knows what happened to you. They know you were in an accident and a coma, and that you came out and you're mostly better now."

"Yeah, except for that organization thing."

The doctors warned that even though she left the hospital with a Rancho Scale of Level VIII, because of the trauma to her brain, there could be some memory or functioning issues. So far, the only thing the occupational therapist noted was Evie's lack of organization.

I smiled. "That's not new, though. I mean, they're trying to fix something you sucked at before. When's your next appointment?"

"Today, after school."

"I'll take you." I sat still for a moment. "And, don't worry. Everyone at school will be fine."

She picked at a corner of the comforter. "I know."

"Think about it this way, okay? This time, they'll be paying attention to you because of what happened to *you*, not something your mom did or said."

She nodded, but didn't lift her gaze from the bed.

"That's not all, is it?"

Evie took a hitching breath and brought her eyes up to meet mine. They were wet with tears and held a sadness I understood in my soul.

I shook my head. "Evie, I'm so sorry. There wasn't anything I could do to save him." Guilt pricked at me as the words left my mouth. *Don't lie to her. You could have done something. You could have stopped him from walking in there.* I shook my head. *No, there wasn't. If I had gone in there, I would be...what? Dead?* I blinked back tears.

"Now there's a hint of orange around you. It feels deceitful, uncertain."

I waved a hand at her. "Stop doing that."

She shrugged. "Can't help it." She squinted at me. "It feels like regret, too."

I bristled. "Look, I'm sorry you're scared, but it's going to be fine, really." I stood up again. "Go get ready."

She didn't move.

"Evie!"

Her eyes sparked. "Not until you tell me what you're hiding about what happened below the courthouse."

"You tell me first," I fired back.

She leveled her gaze at me. "I deserve to know."

Standing there, I was hit with that little bit of truth. She *did* deserve to know, even if she couldn't talk about her experience down there yet. I sat in my desk chair and swiveled it around to face her. "I didn't tell you because I didn't think you were strong enough, yet." *That's a lie.* I closed my eyes and concentrated on silencing the voice in my head.

"Orange."

"Fine, I didn't tell you because what happened to Sam was," I paused, my throat constricting around the words, "my fault."

She shook her head. "No, you told me that the darkness took Sam. That when the thing grabbed him, it let me go."

"That's true, but what I didn't tell you was that it really wanted me."

Evie stared at me for a long minute. "Why didn't you tell me?"

"I should have and I didn't mean to keep this from you, I just…" I let the sentence fade. *You just, what? Didn't want her to hate you for killing her boyfriend?* I swallowed. "I didn't want to make losing Sam any harder than it already was on you."

"The darkness wanted you. That's why it took me. Sam had nothing to do with this."

"Evie, I started to walk into it. I was going to let it take me so it would let you go."

"What happened?" Her eyes were unwavering.

"Sam, he, I was walking and I felt so sad, like I'd lost everything in my life and he was behind me and he told me to run. He, um, pulled me back out of the darkness and he walked forward. Into it." I took a deep breath, "Then it let you go."

"You didn't even try to stop him?"

"Of course I did! I tried, but the man in the bright light pulled me back and told me that it was Sam's choice, his gift to give." I wrapped my arms around my chest. "I'm sorry, Evie."

She stood up, pulling herself straight and tall. "He died because of you."

"Evie, he was already dead."

Electricity shot from her eyes as she stalked across the bedroom. "It should have been me," she said as she walked out the door.

For a moment, I considered letting her comment go. After all, we'd been down this road before. We got mad at each other and then moved along when one of us finally broke down and apologized. I grabbed my towel and stalked toward the bathroom, but then threw it down on the floor.

Not this time. I yanked open my door and walked to her room.

"And another thing…" I said as I walked in.

Evie stood with her back to me, her shoulders hunched as she untangled her shirt and pulled it up over her head. Before she slid her shirt down, I saw a line of scratches running down her back. Four red lines rose up in welts from the base of her neck and ran under her bra strap to the middle of her back.

"Hey!" Evie whirled around, yanking the front of her shirt down. "Knock much?" Her tired eyes narrowed at me.

"What *is* that?" I strode into her room and reached out for the hem of her shirt.

She backed away. "Leave it alone, St. Louis."

"But, what happened?"

Her chin quivered and she shrugged. "I got too close."

"What are you talking about?"

Evie stared at me, her eyes guarded. "You have to promise not to tell."

"Evie!" My voice rose with exasperation. Fear wound a cold hand around my chest.

"Fine, I couldn't sleep last night so I took a walk. I took the spirit board out to the cave."

"Evie!" I reached up and rubbed my forehead. "We decided it wasn't safe to try to contact him anymore. Sam's gone."

She furrowed her brow. "I know, but, I mean, what if it was Grant?"

Her words cut into me. "Listen, I get it, but that's not the same thing. Grant is in Kansas City. Sam's in…well, Sam's not here anymore."

"I think he was in the cave."

I squinted at her. "What are you talking about? Did you see him?"

"No, but I think he came through on the board." She looked down at the floor. "Before it caught on fire, anyway."

I gaped at her. "The board caught on fire?"

"I asked if Sam was there with me. It took a long time, but the planchette started moving really slowly. It felt weak, St. Louis, but it felt like him." A smile played across her mouth. She glanced up at me. "I asked him if he was okay," she swallowed, "and he spelled out, *help me*. Then, the planchette ripped out of my hands and started spinning on the board. I heard a screeching sound coming from one of the tunnels off the cave and then the board burst into flames. I grabbed my coat and ran."

"How'd you get the scratches, Evie?" I whispered.

She hesitated. "As I was climbing out of the cave, I felt this pain in my back. I thought somehow part of the board hit me, you know, was burning me, but then I ran. When I got back to the house, there was a small scratch on my back. I didn't realize it was this bad until this morning."

I stood staring at her. "What were you thinking? Why would you go in there alone?"

She shrugged and smiled. "Because I thought you'd be too chicken to go with me."

She wasn't wrong. Everything about returning to that cave scared me to death.

"Make me a promise. Promise me that you will never go out there alone again? Next time, I'll go with you. We'll bring Andy and Tristan." I held up my hand as the smile spread across her face. "But, we are *not* going out there until we know what we're dealing with, Evie. It's not safe. You get that, right?"

Her smile didn't fade as she nodded. She reached out and punched me lightly in the side of my arm.

"Thanks, St. Louis. Now, go take a shower," she said. "I'm going to put some ointment on the scratches and I'll meet you downstairs."

I took a deep breath as I left her room, Sam's last moments replaying over and over again in my head. *How was I going to tell her that I thought Sam was too far gone to reach out to anyone anymore? That he was gone and we would never be able to get him back?*

CHAPTER 3

I checked the weather on my phone. No more snow expected until the weekend, but the temperatures were going to be frigid for the next few days. "Great," I mumbled, pulling a heavy scarf out of my dresser drawer. I already had on fleece-lined leggings with my warmest boots and a sweatshirt that was at least two sizes too big for me, but it was the warmest thing I owned. I swiped on some mascara and brushed through my long hair before winding it into a loose bun on my head.

Evie's hair dryer turned off in her room and I could hear her knocking around, getting ready. As I put my binder into my backpack, the door to the bathroom opened and Evie walked into my room.

"Ready?" she asked.

"Almost."

"Sorry about earlier."

I dismissed it with a wave of my hand. "It's fine. I get it. Hey, do you know where my science book is?"

Her hand was on the doorknob. "I think it's on the kitchen table."

When she opened my door, the smell of bacon frying wafted into the room. My stomach immediately seized up and let out a growl.

"Is Dad cooking?" I asked.

"Your dad could burn water."

"Shut up. It's bacon. Don't you smell that?"

"You okay, St. Louis?" Evie's brow furrowed.

I placed a hand over my stomach as it growled again. "Come on."

I flipped off the light and Evie closed the door behind us. I followed my nose down the hallway and to the top of the stairs where I stopped, my head cocked to the side.

"What is that?"

"Would you get moving?" Evie walked around me and down the stairs. "I don't want to be late on my first day back. Might miss all the fanfare!"

"You two are up early."

I whirled around. Dad stood in his doorway. His T-shirt was rumpled and his hair was disheveled.

"Sorry I wasn't up. Guess all those sleepless nights in the hospital finally caught up with me."

"Y-you, um, just got up?" I asked. "You haven't been downstairs cooking?"

He squinted at me. "Not unless you'd rather the smoke alarm wake you up. Give me a minute and I'll come down and pop something in the microwave for you if you're hungry."

"Um, no. Thanks anyway." The scent of bacon hung heavy in the air around me, now layered with the rich, buttery aroma of biscuits. "I'm fine. We're leaving in a few minutes. Evie wants to get to school early."

"Have a good first day back. Love you."

"Love you, too, Dad."

He retreated into his room again and I turned to look down the stairs, my nostrils flaring. I walked to the corner landing and then made my way down the remaining steps to the kitchen. Evie sat on the counter, eating a banana with the coffeemaker in brew mode beside her, a stream of black liquid rushing down into the pot.

"Heads up." She threw a granola bar at me and I missed it by a mile.

I bent down to pick it up and saw a pair of legs in orthopedic shoes standing near the stove. Rising up slowly, I stared. An old woman stood with her back to me, an apron tied around her middle as she flipped eggs in a cast iron skillet. She was plump and her gray hair lay in perfect curls along her head. The rustle of a newspaper pulled my gaze over to the table. The paper was held up by two liver-spotted hands and the long, lanky legs of a man jutted out from underneath. The paper rustled again and the man folded it and laid it on the table, revealing his face.

"Grandpa?" I whispered.

"Beef prices fell again. Third time this year." He took a sip of his coffee, the steam rising up and fogging his horn-rimmed glasses along the bottom.

The woman turned and smiled at him, her hand on her hip. "What's the plan for today?"

I hadn't seen them in years, but my grandparents were here.

"You ready?" Evie asked.

I blinked. "Um, yeah. Yeah." I blinked again, not moving.

Evie hopped down from her perch. "I started your car. We'll have to scrape off the windshield." She went out the back door, leaving it open for me.

I watched as my grandma walked over and placed two eggs on my grandpa's plate. She rested her hand on his shoulder for a moment and smiled down at him.

What are they doing here? Why am I seeing them now?

"Come on, St. Louis!" Evie called from the driveway.

I took one last look at my grandparents and then closed the door, my breath hanging on the air as I crossed the snowy driveway to my car.

Evie was already attacking the ice on the windshield. She paused to toss another scraper to me as I approached. "Get the back windows?"

I put my backpack in the backseat and pulled on my gloves. In a matter of minutes, we had the windows cleared off and were in the car, blowing on our frozen hands.

"Did you see anything weird in the kitchen this morning?" I put the car in gear and turned its nose down the driveway.

"I'm assuming you're looking for an answer besides you, right?"

I tossed a scowl her way. "No, I, um, so I think I saw my grandparents in the kitchen."

"That's not anything new for you." She pulled down the visor and checked her face in the mirror.

"I know, I just don't understand why it's the first time I'm seeing them. We've been in the house now for almost three months. I guess I thought if I was going to see them, it would have been before now." I turned onto the road and let out a breath. At least it looked like the snowplow had been through a couple of times and patches of pavement peeked up through the snow. The sun hung low in the sky, spreading weak fingers of pink winter light through the trees. I cleared my throat. "Do you think they're in trouble?"

Evie shook her head and folded the visor back up. "I haven't seen any disruptions in the fabric over the house."

I glanced over at her. "You can still see those? Like the colors?"

"Yeah, the color thing is fading, but I can see disruptions pretty clearly."

We went around a corner in the road and I leaned up over the dashboard, my stomach flip-flopping. A car was in the ditch up ahead. I slowed as we approached. The car lay on its side, almost upside down, its black undercarriage visible and a tire turning slowly.

"Oh my gosh. It must have just happened." I yanked my car over to the shoulder and put it in park. "Call 9-1-1, Evie. I'll see if I can help." I jumped out and ran over to the side of the road. Music came from the car's interior, muffled through the windows. A woman stepped out from around the car, her jacket and dress covered in blood from a gash in her forehead.

"Hey!" I shouted, making my way down the embankment to the car. "Are you okay?"

"Brandon!" The woman called, her attention focused on the car. "Brandon!"

"St. Louis?" Evie's voice was behind me. "What are you seeing?"

I whipped around and looked up at her. "Is the ambulance on the way? I think someone's trapped in the car!"

Evie stood staring at me. When she spoke, the words were slow and deliberate. "There's nothing here, St. Louis. What are you seeing?" she asked again.

I turned around. The woman clawed at the crushed door. There was a man inside, slumped over the steering wheel. A bump in the windshield buckled out from the inside as if someone had thrown a basketball into it. Cracks dripping with blood ran in spider webs out from the bubble. I felt sick.

Taking a deep breath, I walked over to the woman. "Ma'am? Come sit down. The police are on the way."

She didn't look at me but kept clawing at the door, trying to open it. I reached over and tried to pry the door open, but it was no use. The car had landed on the driver's side, pinning the door to the frame. Evie came to stand beside me.

"Help me!" I cried, pulling at the door handle.

Evie placed her hand on my shoulder. "There's a cross there." She pointed to my side. "Nothing more."

I followed her finger in the direction she pointed and saw a white cross with silk flowers adorning it. I stood up walked over to look at it. "Brandon and Beth, we love you," I read, my chest rising and falling as my breath came in bursts. I turned around and looked at Evie. She stood in front of the car, the awful scene playing out behind her.

"I don't know how to help her," I said, my voice breaking with emotion. "She needs help."

"Beth died, St. Louis."

I took a deep breath. "This is a…a vision?"

Evie nodded her head, her brow creased. "I remember this. She worked at the factory with my mom, and Brandon was a clerk at the grocery store. They died here a few years ago. They left a wedding and he was driving too fast."

"But, she got out of the car. She's okay." I walked around Evie and watched the woman yanking at the door, crying. "She's standing right here." I gestured at the figure.

"The newspaper said she died later at the hospital. The accident ruptured her spleen or something. Neither one of them was wearing a seatbelt. Come on, St. Louis, there's nothing you can do for them." Evie took my arm gently.

Numbness spread through my body. I felt drained and the climb up the embankment took more effort than I thought possible. When I got to my car, I rested my hand on the warm hood for a moment, breathing hard.

"Do you want me to drive?" Evie asked.

"Yeah," I mumbled. I climbed into the passenger seat, trying to ignore the cries from the side of the road.

Evie put the car in gear and pulled out onto the road slowly. She drove for several minutes before saying anything. Then, she glanced at me and cleared her throat. "Are you okay?"

I took a deep breath. "Yeah, I'm fine. I just can't help thinking that I'm supposed to help them. That I'm being shown these things because I'm supposed to make it better."

Evie stared straight ahead and didn't say anything.

I went on. "We're not helping anyone. Everyone we've tried to help has come out of it worse than if we never would have tried."

"Now you're being stupid. We helped Mary."

"She's trapped here without Matthias."

"Amalie."

"The doll's back."

Evie sighed. "Okay. We're going to have Andy and Tristan come over tonight and we're going to figure all of this out, okay?"

My chest hurt when I breathed. "Fine." I rolled my head back on the headrest and closed my eyes.

I was sleeping soundly by the time Evie pulled into the school parking lot.

CHAPTER 4

"Morning, sunshine."

My eyes fluttered open. They were immediately assaulted by the brightness of the sun shining on the snow and I fumbled in the glove compartment, looking for my sunglasses. When I found them, I shoved them on my face, blocking out most of the light.

"We're here already?" My voice was gruff and I cleared my throat.

"Yeah. I thought for a minute about leaving you here until lunch," Evie smiled. She looked out the window at the school. "Didn't want you to miss my triumphant return to the land of the living, though."

I sat up and rolled my head around on my shoulders, loosening the muscles. "Thanks," I mumbled. I got out and grabbed my backpack.

Evie tossed me my keys over the roof of the car. "You're okay, aren't you?"

"I'm fine. Just tired." *So tired.*

We headed into school. The second we hit the doors, it was a mad rush. People came from everywhere to talk to Evie. Her cheeks flushed as she answered questions and talked, swept into the crowd heading down the hallway.

"I'll see you later," I called.

She waved at me and I headed to my locker.

"Marissa!" Jessica bombarded me with a huge hug from behind, her ponytail whipping into my face as she hung on my shoulders.

I shrugged her off. She didn't seem to notice.

"Oh my gosh, you poor thing! I just heard! We were in Omaha visiting family and they live way out in the boonies and I wasn't able to get a signal on my phone for, like, days. My grandparents don't even have Wi-Fi at their house, can you believe that? I felt like we were living in the Dark Ages. We didn't get back into town until late last night. We ended up taking Rick with us and so we had to drop him off at his house before we could get home and his mom had to have us in for coffee. We didn't actually get home until about three this morning," she rolled her eyes, "but that's okay because I was able to get, like, three hours of sleep before heading here. When I got to school, you and Evie were all anyone could talk about. I mean, this is the biggest thing that's happened in town for ages and I wasn't even here. Are you all okay?"

I nodded. "We're fine."

"Denise told me she was in a *coma*?" Jessica dropped her voice to a whisper as she said the word. "What happened?"

I talked as I deposited books from my backpack into my locker. "Evie hit her head while we were…out, and the doctors put her into a medically induced coma to allow the swelling to go down in her brain. She got better and now she's back." I shrugged.

"Oh, come on." Jessica turned her head and side-eyed me. "You're talking to *me* here. What *really* happened?"

I thought about everything that transpired while Evie was in a coma. How she was able to walk around town as a spirit and how Sam, the ghost from the courthouse, had helped save her by sacrificing himself to the darkness in the cavern below the town, and how I had helped bridge the gap between the worlds to get Evie's spirit back into her body.

I looked up at Jessica and decided to change the subject. "Grant left for school on Sunday. I already miss him."

Jessica clicked her tongue. "Aw, Marissa, I'm so sorry. It must be awful to be away from him. I know I would just go crazy if Rick and I were that far apart."

I closed my locker and Jessica accompanied me down the hallway, chattering the whole way about what Rick got her for Christmas, her crazy uncle Barnie who insisted on making them all take a family photo in red sweaters, and her grandma's coffee cake, which, while delicious, caused her to gain seventeen pounds if she did anything more than smell it. By the time I got to my first class, I was exhausted. I sat down and folded my arms on the table in front of me, resting my head on the crook of my elbow. The noises of people filing into the classroom were familiar and comforting and I closed my eyes.

"Hey, Marissa."

I opened my eyes.

Kaleb sat in the chair next to me. Defensive end on the football team, he was two hundred twenty pounds of muscle and about the nicest guy I'd ever met.

"Hey," I managed.

"Heard about what happened to your friend over Christmas. Hope she's okay."

I sat up. "She's fine."

He opened his book. "Everyone says you guys were out there looking for the ghost of the Weeping Bridge."

I could feel eyes on my back and the room got quiet. "I, um, we were..." My eyes flitted to the doorway, searching for the teacher. A man in green fatigues walked past the door. Our school had an active JROTC, but most of them wore button down shirts and pants. *Maybe they were training today*. I shivered, thinking of being out in the cold.

"Did you find her?" Leslie hissed, leaning up over her desk. "The ghost?"

My skin felt like it was crawling off my body. I pushed a piece of hair out of my face and turned around in my chair. "We didn't find anything out there. There's a bridge, but there wasn't any ghost." I felt a fierce protection growing in my gut for Mary and her story. Maybe one day I would share it, but until we helped her find her way back to Matthias, it felt wrong to allow anyone else to go out there searching for her, messing with such tragedy. I shrugged. "I guess it's just a story."

"Is that what you guys do?" Leslie asked. "You go out searching for ghosts?"

"Um, kind of." My heart was beating inside my chest and I wished Evie or Andy or Tristan were here. I could imagine they were going through their own respective grilling sessions, though, and I wondered how they were answering. "We hear about ghost stories and we go out to try to confirm them."

"My aunt says her house is haunted," a girl from across the room said. "She gets up every morning and the basement door is open."

"Sounds like they need to check their foundation." Brian raised his eyebrow.

"Shut up. You're only trying to drum up business for your old man."

Kaleb glanced over at me. "You okay?" he asked quietly.

I tried to slump down in my seat.

"Quiet, everyone." Mr. Clark walked in, balancing a coffee cup in one hand and a stack of papers in his other arm. "I graded your essays over the holidays and three words popped into my head: underwhelming, pedestrian, and mediocre." He punctuated each word with the slam of the door, the drop of his bag on the floor, and then the papers on the desk. "Come on, people, we can do better." He pulled the clip off the stack and began handing out papers.

I was thankful that the attention was off me for the moment.

"I think it's pretty cool what you're doing," Kaleb leaned over and whispered. "You'd never catch me messing with ghosts."

I smiled and took the paper Mr. Clark handed me. It was an A and his note at the bottom was full of praise for my word choice and writing style. I looked up and he gave me a small smile before handing Kaleb his paper. I didn't mean to look, but I caught a glance of the large red D scrawled at the top.

Kaleb groaned. "Mr. Clark, Coach is going to kick me off the team if I don't pass your class."

"Then do better," was the response. "That goes for all of you. If you are unsatisfied with your grade, redo it and turn it back in by Monday. I'll take another look and consider raising your grade. For now, turn to page 134 and we're going to talk about the stellar writing of Lorraine Hansberry and her opus, *A Raisin in the Sun*. In this play…"

I leaned over. "I can help you rewrite it if you want."

Kaleb stared down at the paper and then up at me. "You sure? It's a wreck."

I smiled. "Yeah. Want to meet at the…" I hesitated. "Where do people meet in this town to study?"

He shrugged. "And you think I know this why?"

"Fine, come over to my house tomorrow night and we'll work on it."

"Thanks."

"Miss Anderson? Would you mind telling the class about the first act of this play?"

I jerked my head up.

Mr. Clark stared at me over his book, his eyebrow arching up.

I shook my head. "Um, I don't really know it."

He smiled. "Then, would you mind allowing me to do so?"

I could feel the blood rush to my face and tried to ignore the snorts behind me. "Sorry."

The rest of the hour was spent fighting to keep my eyes open. I dug my nails into my palms, bounced my leg, and even resorted to resting one burning eye and then the other. By the time English Comp let out, I was a jittery mess. I wandered down the hall to my next class and then my next one. The day droned on and the pile of homework teachers were assigning was ridiculous. It felt like they had suddenly woken up from winter break and realized that there were only five more months of school to cram in everything in the curriculum.

I was glad when lunch came and I could drop off my books at my locker. I headed into the cafeteria, looking around for my friends as I made my way through the line. They weren't there yet, but the guy in fatigues I saw earlier was sitting out on the picnic table. I looked harder at him. He wore short sleeves and I couldn't imagine how he was dealing with the cold. I paid for my water and apple and made my way over to the door.

Pushing it open, the students at the table nearest the door complained loudly as the icy wind whipped in through the opening.

"Sorry," I muttered and closed it quickly behind me. I moved toward the picnic table. "Hey, you want to come in? You must be freezing."

The man peered up at the building and smiled. He was perched on top of the picnic table, a round green helmet at his side and a vest over his T-shirt.

"Did you hear me?" I took a step closer.

He checked his watch and then leaned his elbows onto his knees, his eyes intent on the people inside the cafeteria. "Come on, Melanie. Where are you?"

I turned to see who he was talking about. The crowd of students inside talked and laughed at their tables.

He reached into his pocket and pulled out a small box. Flipping it open, he stared down at a small diamond ring inside. "Will you marry me, will you marry me, will you marry me?" he muttered. He smiled again and flipped the box closed. "If she says no, you can pull out the but I'm going off to war card. No one could say no to that."

I shivered, the biting air cutting through my sweatshirt. I reached out to touch him on the shoulder. "Sir, are you okay?"

The second my fingertips brushed against the fabric of his shirt, a popping sound reached my ears and the wind rushed around me, whipping my hair. I looked down at the helmet and saw a huge hole blown in the side of it. The man's fatigues turned dirty and wet, ripped in several places and covered in dark splotches. His face grew black with dirt and his eyes became haunted, darting around as the smell of gunpowder rose off him, burning my nose. He blinked and turned my way. I cried out and stepped back. The entire left side of his head was gone and blood covered his matted hair.

"Where's Melanie?" he asked, his eyes finding mine.

"St. Louis, you're going to freeze to death out here!" Evie stood in the doorway, her face full of concern. "What are you doing?"

"Talking to…um, what's your name?"

"Private First Class Daniel Trenton, but everyone calls me Red."

CHAPTER 5

It took some convincing, but Red finally agreed to follow Evie and me inside. We led him through the crowded cafeteria and down the hall into the basement art room. Andy and Tristan were already there.

"Hey, Patton! Figured you could use a break from your celebrity status," Andy called out. He wrapped an arm around her shoulder and hugged her. "Glad you're back," he said quietly.

"What's going on?" Tristan looked at me with concern in his eyes. "You seem upset."

"She has a ghost with her," Evie answered.

"He was sitting outside on the picnic table." I sat down heavily in a desk and motioned for Red to do the same.

He shook his head and stood in the corner of the room, his helmet thankfully on his head, hiding most of the horrible injury underneath. His eyes swept around the room sadly. "I remember this was Mrs. Hoffman's room when I went to school here. Everything's changed." His voice held a sadness in it that broke my heart.

"Who is he?" Tristan asked.

"Private First Class Daniel Trenton. He says his friends called him Red."

"Private First Class? In the Army?" Andy asked.

"Yes, I enlisted the day I turned eighteen."

"Wait a minute," I turned to look at Red. "You can hear him?"

"A bit. The sound is muffled, but I can make out most of the words."

I shook my head and put it in my hands.

"St. Louis?"

"I'm fine. I'm just trying to wrap my brain around all of this. He says he can hear you, but you come through muffled and he can't pick up every word. Red, can you see them?"

He tilted his head to the side. "I can make out a shadow if I concentrate. There are a couple shadows, um, no, three."

"You're right." I pointed. "This is Andy, Tristan, and Evie."

Evie raised her hand in a wave.

"How about me?" I asked. "Am I muffled, too?"

He shook his head. "You come through clearly. I can see you and hear you." His voice dropped a notch. "Can you please tell me what's going on?"

"I think you're a ghost. There's a terrible injury to your head and you are at Culvers Grove High School. Do you remember anything about what happened to you?"

"I didn't remember anything until you were outside talking to me. Before that, I was, well, here. I walked through the hallway and out to the table. Then I waited there to propose to Melanie." He smiled. As he spoke, a drop of red blood snuck out from under his helmet and ran down his cheek. "Now, I remember other...things."

I watched as it splashed onto the collar of his shirt, spreading into a dark blotch on the dirty material. I took a shaking breath and told them what Red said.

He gazed at me and leaned against the counter. "Now I remember enlisting with the Army when I turned eighteen, and I remember that I wanted to ask Melanie to marry me before I left for Fort Leonard Wood."

I smiled, rubbing my temples. "Did you ask her?"

His eyes met mine. His brow furrowed. "I don't know. I don't remember. I came to school and I was here waiting to ask her, and then, I was headed to basic training and then I was in Vietnam."

"Vietnam?"

"Yeah, my tour started on January 8, 1969. First Battalion, 21st Field Artillery Regiment stationed near Tây Ninh Province, South Vietnam."

"Red, I think you were killed there. There's a huge hole in your helmet and your, um, head," I motioned to my own, "is really messed up."

"I remember that now. My squad was out and we were ambushed. I remember shots fired and we tried to hide in the bush, but there were too many of them and we couldn't see them…" He stopped and looked up at me. "Then I felt something hit my head and everything stopped. I closed my eyes and when I woke up, I was here at school, and I was waiting to ask Melanie to marry me." He turned sad eyes to me. "Do you think she would have said yes?"

"So, he was reliving a happy memory over and over again until you touched him?" Tristan asked when I told them what Red said.

I nodded, a lump growing in my throat.

"Does he remember anything else?" Andy asked.

A tear escaped and ran down my cheek, hot and wet. "Red, what else do you remember?"

His eyes took on a wistful quality. "I remember waiting to ask Melanie to marry me the day before I went to basic training. I remember the people I met there. The training. The feeling of being so far away from home even though I wasn't even across the ocean yet."

As he talked, I translated in a hushed tone for the group.

"I remember shipping out, and when we landed, it was like walking down the steps into a sauna. The heat and humidity knocked the breath right out of me, which was a good thing, because the next thing I noticed was the smell. It was a mix of rotting vegetation and sh..." he blushed and cleared his throat. "...excrement. I tried breathing through my mouth, but it wasn't any use. It was like walking next to the cafeteria dumpsters in the summer." He swiped a hand across his forehead. "The kids ran up asking for things the minute we stepped off the plane and I was 'GI number one' because I gave them all a piece of candy. They took us to base camp and I met a lot of guys there. Good guys. Austin, Mickey, and Blue." Red shook his head. "Charlie got them all the first month I was there. I made it to May before I bit the big one."

We all sat quietly for a moment.

"What can we do to help him?" Tristan asked. He walked over and placed a hand on my shoulder. "I'm sorry, Red. That sounds awful."

Red's eyes widened. "I can hear him."

I looked up. "You can?"

Red nodded.

"Say something else, Tristan," I directed.

He took a step back and said, "Um, I'm sorry that you died."

I stared at Red. He shook his head.

"Wait a minute. Come back here." I reached out and grabbed Tristan's hand. "Try it now."

Tristan repeated his sentence.

"I can hear him, now. It's still muffled, but I can make out the words better."

"Can you see him?" My voice trembled.

Red squinted. "I think so. He's wearing a blue shirt and he has blond hair."

"You're right. Tristan, he can see and hear you some when you touch me."

"Do it the other way now," Tristan said. "Touch him and see if we can see him."

I swallowed and shivered, remembering the pain when I touched Evie before. "I'm scared."

"We're right here, St. Louis. If anything happens, we've got you."

"Okay. Red, we're going to try something. Since you can see Tristan when he touched me, we're going to try it the other way." I stood up and held out my hand.

Red looked down at it. He took a step forward and reached out his hand.

The second our palms made contact, I felt electricity move through my arm.

"You okay, Anderson?"

"Um, yeah. I can feel the electricity, but it's not as bad as it was with Evie. It's duller somehow." I turned to look at Red. "Say something."

"Hello, my name is Daniel Trenton."

I whipped my head around to look at the group. "So?"

Andy's face was white. "That was trippy. I heard *hello* and *Daniel*. It was sort of a whisper. What'd you guys hear?"

Evie and Tristan said they heard the same.

"What happens if you hold Tristan's hand and Red's at the same time?" Evie asked.

"Gee, I love this game of let's experiment on Marissa," I mumbled. I reached out my other hand toward Tristan.

He took it and the electricity from Red's hand amped up a notch, spreading cold pinpricks into my arm and shoulder. Tristan's hand sent out electricity, too, a hot buzzing sensation.

"I see him," Tristan whispered. "He's a shadow, but I can see him. He has on a helmet and he's wearing green. Can you hear me, Red?"

"I can. Can you hear me?"

"Yes! Almost every word."

I felt my energy draining from the top of my head. My eyelids drooped and I swayed a bit on my feet. "Let go, please," I whispered, barely moving my mouth.

Tristan and Red let go quickly and each took a step back from me.

"Are you okay?" Tristan asked.

"So…tired…" I managed before I collapsed on the floor.

When my eyes opened again, I was sitting in a chair, my head propped up on a table in the back corner of the library. I rubbed my eyes. Andy sat across from me, scrolling through his phone.

"Welcome back, Anderson," he said, not looking up.

"How long was I out?"

"About forty-five minutes."

"I missed class."

"Evie's getting notes for you."

I sighed and clicked my dry tongue against the roof of my mouth. Andy slid a bottle of water across the table. I caught it and took a long drink before trying to speak again.

"Where's Red?"

Andy widened his eyes at me and shrugged.

"That's right. You wouldn't know. Sorry." I looked around at the quiet room. "How did you get me up here?"

"You ever see *Weekend at Bernie's*?"

I laughed. "Shut up. No, you didn't."

Andy's gaze was unwavering.

"Oh my God, you did."

"We took the back stairs. Hardly anyone saw us."

"*Hardly* anyone?"

He chuckled. "A couple of freshmen girls. They were so excited that Evie stopped to talk to them that they didn't pay any attention to us."

I smiled. "You're ridiculous."

"Pretty handy in a pinch, though. I've got the, you know, mad skills and all." He stood up and threw the strap of his backpack over his shoulder. "You ready to get moving? Bell's gonna ring in a few and I want to get you to class before I'm late to mine."

I stood up slowly, testing my legs while holding onto the edge of the table. They seemed sturdy enough, but I felt completely drained.

"I could sleep for hours," I said as he held out his arm for me. "Thanks."

"Don't mention it."

"Are we going to talk about what happened in the art room?"

The bell rang and Andy shook his head. "Not here. Not now. Tristan and I are coming over later. We can talk then."

He walked me through the hallways and dropped me off at my last class of the day. I spent the entire class trying everything I could to stay awake, counting down the minutes until the bell rang. I left with pinch marks on the skin of my left arm and a pounding headache.

Evie met me by my locker and took my backpack from me. She closed the locker door and looked at me. "You look like crap, St. Louis."

"Thanks," I mumbled and fished my keys out of the bottom of my purse. "You drive?"

She caught the keys when I tossed them to her and walked with me out to the car. I tumbled into the passenger side and used my coat as a blanket across my chest. Evie turned the heat up full blast but I was still shivering when she pulled out of the parking lot and onto the road to town.

"Do you want me to take you home?" she asked finally.

I shook my head, my teeth chattering. "You'll be late for your appointment. I'll be okay. I just need to rest."

She pulled the car into town and we passed the Post Office and the diner. Several cars were parked along the street. She stopped at a stop sign and I watched a little boy and girl running around the yard of a house through my half open eyelids.

"They should put a coat on," I mumbled.

Evie shot me a strange look and then moved on down the street. A woman in a long dress and hat with feathers sprouting from the hatband walked along the sidewalk next to us for a while, two bags swinging from her gloved hands.

"Is she going to a costume party?" I asked, and then allowed my eyes a long blink. When my eyelids raised again, I sat up straight and called out, "Stop!"

Evie slammed on the brakes and the car came to a stop mere inches from a man walking across the street. He didn't even look over, but kept walking, stepping up onto the sidewalk, and then disappearing into a building on the corner.

"What the heck, St. Louis?" Evie glanced in the rearview mirror. "Sorry," she murmured to the car that honked behind her. She started driving again.

"Didn't you see that guy? You almost ran over him!"

Evie looked over at me. "Something really weird is going on. You're seeing all sorts of things that aren't there."

I bristled. "You're honestly telling me that you didn't see anyone walking in front of the car just now?"

"No!" Evie drove along. "I didn't see the car this morning or the kids without coats or the man you almost got me rear-ended for."

I peered out the window. "What about him? Do you see him?" I pointed to a man in a ratty pair of jeans heading into the local bar.

"Of course I see him."

"Her?" I pointed to a woman rushing to her car with a bag of groceries.

"Um, yeah, I see her." Evie parked the car in front of the office building adjacent to the hospital.

My hand flew to my mouth.

"What's wrong?"

"Oh my gosh, Evie." I pointed out the windshield, my blood running cold. Tears burned my eyes. "There are so many…"

CHAPTER 6

"St. Louis, wake up!"

I pulled myself upright and looked around, confusion knotting my stomach. "W-where am I?"

Evie cocked her head to the side, and then spoke to someone in the room. "Well, at least she's okay enough to sound like a bad actor." She turned back to me. "Seriously, you couldn't come up with anything better than that?" She smiled, but it belied the worry I saw in her eyes.

I shook my head and closed my eyes, taking a deep, centering breath. When I opened them again, I realized I was in my own room in my own bed. Evie sat cross-legged on the end of it and Andy and Tristan sat on the futon.

"Hey, guys," I said.

"How's it, Anderson?"

"Are you feeling okay?"

"I could use a glass of water."

Tristan stood up with a groan. "Coming right up." He left the room and I tried to swing my legs out of bed, but Evie's weight kept them trapped under the covers.

Her eyes fixed on me. "How are you feeling?"

"Honestly?" I leaned back against my headboard. "Awful." My fingers tingled and my chest hurt. I thought I might be suffering from a heart attack, but statistics were on my side seeing as how I was only sixteen and not a likely candidate for heart disease yet. I gripped my hands into fists for a moment. "I feel like I ran a marathon."

Tristan came in and handed me a tall glass of ice water. I grabbed it and took a few grateful gulps, allowing the cool liquid to coat my shaking insides. The water splashed into my empty stomach, and it started to growl.

Tristan smiled and tossed a granola bar to me. "Figured you'd be hungry."

"Thanks," I said, ripping into the wrapper and devouring the bar.

"What, you didn't bring one for…" Andy started. He grabbed the granola bar Tristan held out. "And, that's why I love you."

Tristan turned to me again. "Evie said you passed out in the car."

"Yeah, one minute you were yelling at me for almost hitting a man that wasn't there, and then, we pulled up to the hospital and your eyes got really wide and you said something about there being so many of them."

"What did you see, Marissa?"

I looked into Tristan's eyes. "It was awful." I shuddered. "There were people everywhere. They were bleeding and dying…" I took a shuddering breath. "There were men and *boys* there. Little kids." A tear escaped and wound its way down my cheek. I pulled up the edge of my sheet and wiped my eyes, leaving a black mascara smudge on the material.

"Here." Tristan handed me a tissue.

"Thanks."

We sat there quietly for a moment.

Tristan sat down heavily in the desk chair. "The hospital was built on the site of one of the battles of the Mormon War of 1838. Have you heard of it?"

I shook my head.

"At that time, the Latter-Day Saints were being driven out of Missouri by an 'extermination order' from the governor. There were several skirmishes in this area that forced the Mormons to relocate. About forty settled here in Culvers Grove, and in the fall of that year, a band of vigilantes arrived at their settlement and attacked. A mill was located where the hospital is now and after sending the women and girls to hide in the surrounding woods, the men and boys attempted to find a defense point from the mob in the mill. Unfortunately, they were shot through the large gaps between the logs. About seventeen were killed that day, mostly men and boys."

"How do you *know* all of this stuff?" Evie asked. She turned to Andy. "He's like a walking encyclopedia."

Andy shrugged.

Tristan smiled. "I think it's interesting. Didn't you ever wonder what that big round monument was for?" He looked around. "I'll assume from the silence that none of you have noticed that there was a grindstone with a plaque in that space? Anyway, it was a memorial to the people that lost their lives there."

"But, why am I seeing them?" I asked, my voice small. "I was at the hospital a dozen times while Evie was there and I didn't see anything. Why now?"

"Patton says you've been losing it all day. She said you were like a crazy person this morning on the way to school."

"His word, not mine," Evie said.

"I don't know what's happening to me. I'm having visions of people that are dead *all the time*." I reached up and rubbed my forehead. "I was just getting a handle on it and now it's like the veil has been ripped off and I can't control when I see things."

"Say that again." Evie leaned toward me, her eyes sparking.

"It's, um, like the veil's been ripped off and I can't control when I see things."

"Do you remember New Year's Eve?"

I nodded. It was the last time I saw Grant before he left for college. *He's only been gone a few days.*

"Don't be sad. You'll get to see him soon," Evie whispered. "On the porch that night, you said something changed, something felt different. You started seeing all sorts of weird people that weren't there."

I nodded again. "I remember. We were getting ready to go back in the house and get your wheelchair when I heard this big boom that made my ears pop. A wind came up and then I saw that woman on the porch next door. It was like she had been plucked right out of the 1950s."

"You said you saw something in the window across the street."

"Yeah, a couple was playing cards at the dining room table and there was another man and lady, dressed in Victorian clothes, dancing. There was also a woman in a long prairie dress, rocking a baby in her arms." I shook my head. "I don't know why they were all there."

"What if only one of them really is there?" Andy asked.

"What do you mean?"

He scooted up to the edge of the futon. "Patton, what did you see through the window?"

She furrowed her brow. "The couple sitting at the table playing cards. Why?"

"Because, I think they are the only *living* people in the house. I think Anderson's seeing both living people and nonliving people, at the same time."

I let the enormity of what he was suggesting settle on me. It felt like a weight and I suddenly couldn't breathe.

"That makes complete sense," Evie chimed in. "That's why you're so tired all the time, St. Louis. Remember when you first started seeing the visions? They would drain you. You got a little better at keeping that from happening, but if there's no filter, then your ability is on all the time. Draining you. That's why you fell asleep in the car at the hospital."

"Oh, man, did you miss your appointment with the OT?"

Evie smiled. "Seriously? They're treating me for an organization problem. They have to expect that I'll flake on them at least a few times. You know, brain injury and all." She crossed her eyes.

"I'm sorry." I put the glass on my nightstand.

"Marissa, if you're open to the spirit world all the time, it's going to be hard for you to tell what's real and what's not," Tristan said.

I pressed my lips together. "I already thought of that. It's going to suck."

"We'll stay with you at all times, and we'll try to stay away from places with ghosts." Evie patted my leg.

"That's impossible." I swallowed. "They're everywhere."

Tristan got out his phone and scrolled through his apps. "I have everyone's class schedule here," he said.

"Of *course* you do," Andy teased.

Tristan ignored him. "Okay, Evie, you have the mornings before school and time after school. Andy and I can take turns walking you through the halls and make sure you get to class." He turned to Andy. "Can you take her after lunch?"

My blood boiled and I yanked my feet out from under Evie, sending her sprawling to the side.

"Hey!" she squawked.

I placed my bare feet on the rug near my bed and stood up. "I refuse to be babysat." I said, hoping my voice didn't waver. "This is ridiculous. I'll be fine at school. Red's the only one there, and as for everything else, I've gotten control of it before, I can do it again."

Evie stared at me for a moment, and then turned to Tristan. "I can take her after lunch. We'll go through the back stairs to the old weight room and cut across the parking lot to the other side. Can you have the door open for us?"

"Stop ignoring me."

"Sure, I'll make sure I have my Trig book with me when I go to lunch. That should give me enough time to get up there to meet you."

"I know you hear me."

"And I can walk her to her car after school," Andy offered. "That way, if she's really tired, I can carry her." He held up a scrawny arm and made a fist. "I've been working out."

Tristan snorted. "Yeah, lifting a fork to your mouth. Lift, repeat, lift, repeat." He mimed the motion of eating.

Andy cocked his head to the side. "Did you just make a joke? Guys, I think he did!"

Tristan flopped down on the futon next to Andy and flumped him with a pillow.

"Fine, since no one wants my opinion, I'm going downstairs." I put on my mangled bunny slippers and padded to the door. My hand was on it when I remembered that my grandparents were downstairs in the kitchen. I let out a growl and turned around, resting my back against the door as I slid down to the floor.

"What's wrong?"

I narrowed my eyes at Evie. "My dead grandparents are hanging out in the kitchen. I don't really feel like seeing them and then face planting on the linoleum."

"Wow, St. Louis, you should really try to dial it down a notch."

"You try dealing with all this," I snapped.

"Oh, come off it. A week ago, I was dealing with being *dead.*"

"You weren't dead," I mumbled sullenly. I looked up. "Don't you guys understand what this means? This means that I won't be able to go anywhere without being afraid that I'm going to talk to someone who isn't there, or see something terrifying, or fall asleep in the middle of class..."

"Well, everyone expects that in Creavy's class anyway," Andy said.

Evie smoothed the bedspread and patted it. "Listen, when you're done with the pity party, maybe we can start talking about what we're going to do about all of this."

I felt all the fight go out of me. "Fine." Standing up, I made my way back to the bed and sat down, the heat creeping up my neck. "Sorry I lost it there."

"We get it," Tristan said, leaning around Andy to make eye contact with me. "We really do, but this isn't the end of the world." He nodded his head. "What we need is a plan."

Everyone stared at me.

"You're right. We need to take stock of what we can do to help everyone."

"Including you," Tristan said.

I got up and retrieved a notebook and pen off my desk. I opened it to the first blank page and clicked my pen as I sat down on the floor.

"So, who's first?" I asked.

"We need to help Hannah. You saw the text her mother sent us before New Year's. She's terrified."

I wrote Hannah's name on the first line.

"But she hasn't reached out to us since then," Andy said.

"She said her husband would be in town until after the beginning of the year and we weren't to contact her before that."

Tristan looked at me. "Do you think she'll get in touch with you?"

I considered. "Yeah, I think she will."

"Any idea what we're going to do to help her?"

I shook my head. "I'll text Kristen today and see if she'll let us come out and talk to her again."

"What about Old Man Dietrich?"

"What about Mary?"

Andy and Tristan spoke at the same time and then swung their eyes to me.

I chewed on the top of the pen. "I'm not sure what we're going to do for either of them. I know it sounds harsh, but as long as they're not bothering anyone right now, I think they have to go down on the bottom of the list." I wrote Theodore and Mary, my hand shaking as I wrote the last one. "Did that sound harsh?" I asked.

"No, I don't think anyone's moved into Old Man Dietrich's house yet and Mary's house is, well..." Tristan trailed off.

Andy shrugged. "It's destroyed. Annihilated. A pile of rubble."

I told them about the dream I had while Evie was in the hospital, how all of the ghosts we *helped* showed up asking for me to help them, to put them to rest.

"We didn't do anything to help them, and now there's Red." My pen hovered above the paper. "How do we help *him*?"

"Maybe we have to find Melanie?"

"His girlfriend?" I furrowed my brow. "She'd have to be like..."

"Almost seventy."

"If we find her, we can take her back to the school and Marissa can do that bridge thing and let her see and talk to Red." Andy gave me the thumbs up sign. "That was seriously the coolest thing I've seen in a long time."

"Would she even want to see him? What if she's moved on?" Tristan asked. "Wouldn't that just bring up bad memories from her past?"

"Evie and I will work on finding out if Melanie is still around. Maybe my dad knows about her." I wrote Red's name at the top of the list. "We have to find something to help him move on. It's my fault he knows that he's a ghost. It's my fault that he's hurting."

"How do you figure?" Andy asked.

"He was perfectly fine. He didn't even look hurt and then I talked to him, touched him, and everything came crashing down."

"Do you think that's what's happening with some of the ghosts you're seeing?" Tristan asked. "I mean, not all the spirits are reaching out to you, right?"

"Right."

"Maybe some are happy to keep reliving a good memory over and over again. Maybe that's why you see some people hanging around and they're not interacting with the living."

I squinted at him. "All the ghosts we've dealt with have been unhappy. They've been searching for something, and that's why I could see them before. They were *trying* to reach out to me!"

"They were trying to reach out to anyone," Andy corrected. "You were the only one able to hear them."

"Evie?" I spun my head around to look at her. "Have you seen any disturbances in the fabric over our house?"

She sat looking at the list in my lap.

"Evie?"

Her gaze lifted and she stared at me with tear-filled eyes. "Why isn't he on the list?" she whispered.

"Who?"

A tear slipped out. "Sam. Why isn't *he* on your list?"

I looked over at the guys. Andy squirmed uncomfortably and Tristan got up to sit next to Evie on the bed.

He reached out to take her hand. "Honey, I don't think we could save Sam now. I don't think *anything* can save him." He took a deep breath. "I'm sorry."

"Write his name down." She swiped at the tear that was gliding down her cheek.

I stared at her.

"Write it down!" she shouted.

"O-okay, Evie," I said as I scratched his name at the bottom of the list. "Look, it's there. When we figure all of this other stuff out, we'll try to find Sam, okay?"

She started to cry. Her shoulders shook and she sniffled as she buried her face in the shoulder of Tristan's fluffy blue sweater.

Andy and I exchanged a look. I read my own thoughts in his eyes:

He's too far gone. Nothing can save him now.

CHAPTER 7

I stood at the top of the stairs and watched as Evie walked Andy and Tristan down into the kitchen. I smelled bacon cooking again and leaned down to see if I could see any movement in the room. I heard my grandfather talking and then my grandma answering him. Their voices were drowned out by Evie's as she said goodbye to the guys. She came around the corner and jumped when she saw me at the top of the stairs.

"You scared me!" She climbed the stairs and stood looking at me. "What are you doing?"

I pressed my lips together. "I think my grandparents are down there."

"If it helps, I don't see any disturbance over the house," she said quietly.

"Which means they're happy."

"Do you want to go down and see them?"

I shook my head. "Not tonight." The exhaustion was setting in again.

"You need to eat."

"I know." My gaze didn't leave the staircase.

Evie rolled her eyes. "Come on." She plucked at my sleeve and started down the hallway toward the front of the house. Stopping, she looked back. "Come on. We'll go down into the living room and you can stay there. I'll get you something to eat from the kitchen."

"Is my dad down there?" I asked.

"Yeah, he's in his office."

I took a deep breath. I followed Evie downstairs into the living room and threw myself on the couch. She pulled a blanket from the back of the chair and laid it over my legs.

"What do you want to eat?" she asked.

I yawned. "I don't care. Whatever's easiest."

"Sure." She stepped around my feet and went to the office door. "Want anything to eat, Mr. A?"

"Let me finish up what I'm working on here and then I'll come in and help," he said.

"It's okay." Evie backed away from the door slowly. "*Don't* let him come in and help me," she said to me as she passed.

I closed my eyes and leaned my head back on the couch. I wasn't sure how long I lay there, but as the smells of baking pork chops and stuffing intermingled with the phantom scent of bacon hanging heavy in the air, I felt the couch cushion sink next to me. I opened my eyes.

Dad put his arm around my shoulders and squeezed. "Hey, you feeling okay?"

I nodded.

"First day at school can be rough after the break," he mused, pulling a butterscotch out of his shirt pocket. He offered it to me. "Want one?"

I shook my head and let my eyes close again.

He smiled and patted my knee. Grunting, he stood up and stretched. "Smells good in there, huh?"

He headed into the kitchen and I let my head fall back onto the couch again.

Evie shook me awake. "I'm sorry. He said that we should eat in the kitchen. Something about a family night." She shrugged.

I wiped the sleep from my eyes, managing to smear more of my mascara onto my hand. I looked up at Evie.

She raised her eyebrows. "Nice look."

"Shut up." I pushed my body off the couch and stood in the middle of the living room, the blanket wrapped around me. "I have to go in there." Resolve coated my voice.

"I could tell him that you got sick and bring you some food later."

I folded the blanket and placed it back on the chair. "I'll be fine. If you see me start to fade, though…" I left the sentence hanging in the air.

"I know. I'll make an excuse and we'll get you upstairs."

"Thanks, for, you know, being so understanding."

"No worries. Sorry for being a basket case earlier."

"Now, you're only apologizing for that one time you were a basket case, right? I don't get an apology for all the other times?"

She narrowed her eyes at me and then went to the kitchen. I followed behind.

When I crossed the threshold into the room, I was almost overwhelmed with the vision of the past. Grandpa sat at the table, reading the newspaper and Grandma bustled around the room, chattering as she cooked. Evie and Dad stood at the counter, filling plates. The platter of pork chops and bowl of stuffing sat directly on top of Grandma's spectral sheet of biscuits waiting to go into the oven. Grandma wiped her hands on her apron and moved through Evie to retrieve them from the counter. I watched as her spirit disappeared into Evie as the more alive version overtook the ghostly apparition.

I held my breath. *What if touching Evie brought Grandma out of the memory and made her as sad as I'd made Red?* I watched until my grandma reappeared as she moved to put the biscuits in the oven. Then I let my breath out. *So, apparently, it's only me that breaks ghosts. Awesome.* I stepped into the kitchen, careful to avoid touching my grandma as I filled my plate quickly and went over to the table. I sat on the far side, wedged up against the wall and cut into my pork chop.

Dad stared at me for a moment, then shook his head and started eating. "How was school today?" he asked between bites.

"It was good," Evie said, keeping an eye on me while she ate. "Everyone wanted to know all about my accident. That was pretty cool." She smiled.

I watched my grandparents carefully, aware that my energy was draining. I took a deep breath and focused, trying to ebb the flow of energy as it was siphoned out of my body. Grandma walked over to her husband and placed a gentle hand on his shoulder. Her faded eyes filled with love as she looked at him. Warmth radiated out from them and I noticed something I hadn't that morning. If I held my head just right, I could see a mist of sorts building around them, wrapping them in a white cloud. It went away when I looked directly at it, but if I tilted my head and squinted, I could make it out.

I realized that the kitchen had gone quiet and glanced up at my dad and Evie. They were both staring at me. I quickly cut a piece of meat and put it in my mouth.

Dad jerked his chin in my direction. "How did the space cadet over there do today?"

Evie smiled. "She was good. She made a new friend."

"Oh, yeah?" Dad shoved a bite into his mouth and followed it with a gulp of water.

"Um, yeah." I looked pointedly at Evie. "Kaleb is coming over tomorrow night so I can help him rewrite his English Comp paper. He has to pass the class so he can stay on the football team."

"That's not the only new friend she made."

I widened my eyes at her. *Why?*

She smiled.

I curbed my frustration and shoved a huge forkful of stuffing into my face. "It's not exactly someone I met, but it's someone I heard about. Did you ever hear of a Daniel Trenton?"

"Huh." He stopped eating and tented his hands, resting his chin on them and regarding me over his fingers. "The name sounds familiar. Who is he?"

"He would have been a lot older than you. Someone was talking about how he died in the Vietnam War."

Dad sat back and used the napkin to wipe his mouth. "You know, I *do* remember him. He was killed a few years before I was born. Dad used to run with him in high school. He was a football star, promising athlete, but he dropped out of school and signed up for the armed forces the day he turned eighteen." He got up to put his plate in the sink, then turned and leaned against the counter. Grandma sat down in the chair he vacated and held her hand in Grandpa's as she bowed her head to say grace. As soon as I looked at them, I felt my energy pulling away from me again.

"Um, do you know if he was married?" Evie asked, casting a worried glance in my direction.

Dad furrowed his brow. "Dad said that he dated Melanie Turner."

"Where is she now?"

"I believe she still lives here. You know that house right on the outskirts of town, that godawful gold colored one with the green shutters?"

I raised my eyebrows and smiled at Evie. *She was here. In Culvers Grove!*

Dad sighed. "She's not a Turner anymore, though. Mom and Dad used to play bridge with them on Friday nights at their house in town. I hung out with their son, Thomas. He died in an accident right after we graduated..." Dad's voice faded off as he turned inward to his memories.

"Their last name?" Evie asked.

He shook his head and turned away to pour a cup of coffee. "I can't think of it right now. Marissa, you do the dishes tonight since Genevieve cooked?"

"Um, sure," I said, finishing off the last bite of my dinner. "It was really good," I said.

"It was. Listen, I've got a few more hours of work on a case I have to get to. You guys go to bed early so you're ready for school tomorrow."

"Night, Dad," I said.

"Night."

I held onto the edge of the table and looked up at Evie.

She smiled and motioned toward the stairs. "Go on. I'll clean up."

I shot her a grateful glance and made my way slowly up the stairs.

When she was done with the dishes, she came into my room and sat on the edge of my bed. I could barely keep my eyes open.

"It worked," she said.

"What?"

"Distracting you. When you weren't paying attention to your grandparents' ghosts, you didn't lose energy as fast, did you?"

I shook my head once. "Thank you."

"Don't mention it. I'm headed to bed. You okay?"

I blinked and stared blankly at her, my eyes drooping. "What?"

"You know, you're crap for hanging out with, St. Louis." She smiled and turned out the light as she left my room.

I was asleep before I heard the door to her room close.

CHAPTER 8

The next morning, I woke up feeling much better. I had energy and hopped out of bed with a smile. I was in the shower when I heard the door open.

"Hey, I'm in here!" I shouted. There was no answer and I rinsed the shampoo out of my hair. A breeze fluttered the shower curtain and I took a sharp breath in. "Evie?" No answer. I finished up and grabbed the towel from the curtain rod. Wrapping it around me, I whipped the curtain back and fixed a stern look on my face. "You know, if you need to use the bathroom, it's customary to knock…" The sentence died in my throat when I saw my breath hanging in a cloud in the air. I shivered and walked over to the mirror. Swiping a hand across the wet surface, I saw a shadow standing behind me. I squinted and leaned forward, my breath catching in my throat. *Sam?* I whirled around. The bathroom was empty. I looked back in the mirror and only saw my reflection. The steam covered me and the cold was gone.

"Hey! I need in there, St. Louis! Hurry up!"

"Um, almost done." I wrapped my towel more tightly around me and put on some deodorant. Before I left the bathroom, I checked the mirror again. Nothing. Sighing, I unlocked the door to Evie's room and knocked on it to let her know I was done. Heading into my room, I got dressed and blew my hair dry, wrapping it in a loose bun on the top of my head. I tried to ignore the smell of bacon wafting up through the space between the door and the floor. When the scent began to coat my tongue, I walked over and shoved the wet towel into the space.

Sitting down on my bed, I unplugged my phone from the charger and pulled up Kristen's phone number. I stared down at the photo of the doll she sent me before New Year's. *How did the doll get back to the house? Moreover, why was she there now?* I swept my finger over the keyboard, letting Kristen know that we would be available to come out to her house on Friday evening. I watched the screen for a moment and then shoved my phone into my pocket. *Her husband's probably eating breakfast with them.*

I heard Evie slamming things around in the bathroom and judged that she would be ready in about ten minutes. I chewed on my thumbnail. *Had I seen Sam in the mirror?* Well, I knew it wasn't really him. It was probably my guilt that made me see him. I decided I would try to go to the courthouse with Evie that afternoon to see if I could pick up on any trace of him. I smiled when she knocked on my door. Kicking the towel out of the way, I opened it and tossed my car keys at Evie.

"You drive. I'm going to keep my eyes closed on the way to school."

"Um, sure." She started down the stairs.

"I'll head out the front door. Drive around and I'll meet you there."

I went down the front stairs and stopped by the office to say goodbye to Dad, and then I stood out on the front porch until Evie came around in my car. Hopping in, I threw my backpack on the floor and buckled up.

"Okay," I said. "Eyes are closing now. Let me know when we get to school." *I hope this works.*

The car lurched as Evie headed up the driveway. I reached over with a blind hand and turned on the radio. I tried to gauge how far we'd driven by the sound of the wheels on the road and the turns we made. When we got to the curve in the road where I'd seen the accident, I squeezed my eyes tighter. As we passed, I caught the sound of screaming through the window and clamped hands over my ears until we passed.

When we got to school, Evie parked and tapped me on the shoulder. "We're here."

I opened my eyes.

"How do you feel?"

"I feel okay. A little drained, but not bad. Thanks for driving."

She stared up at the school. "There's a spike of disturbance over it this morning that wasn't there yesterday."

"Red?" I asked.

She watched me with wary eyes. "What if you see him in there?"

I sighed and looked at the school. "I'll try to ignore him. I don't think he should know yet that we're trying to find his fiancée until we make sure she's open to seeing him."

Evie rolled her eyes. "*That's* going to be a fun conversation."

"Maybe we can try to track her down after we go by the courthouse this afternoon."

Evie stared at me.

I laughed. "Yeah, I'll go and see if I can find any trace of Sam there." I lowered my voice and spoke earnestly. "Promise me you'll be okay with whatever we find?"

She nodded, her mouth twitching with the smile she was trying to keep from her face.

"And, promise that if I don't feel him there, you'll let him go?"

This time, she nodded, the smile completely fading from her features. "I promise." She threw her arm around my shoulders as we walked toward the front doors of the building. "Thanks, St. Louis."

I walked into English Comp and sat down at the table. The bank of windows looked out on the road that passed by the front of the school. I watched cars pass along, some turning into the parking lot and whipping into spaces, their owners running to beat the first bell. The chair beside me moved a bit and I said, "Hey, Kaleb." Looking over, I jumped.

Red sat in the chair, his eyes full of despair. "Everything's so different," he said.

"Um, like what?" I asked, trying to mask my question by digging in my backpack for my book.

"It isn't like when I went to school here." He pulled on my core of energy, siphoning it off.

I placed my hand over my mouth and spoke quietly. "Red, we're trying to figure out a way to help you, but you have to be patient, okay?"

"What are you going to do?"

"I don't know yet, but we have an idea. In the meantime, you have to stay away from me, Red."

His eyes registered hurt. "But you're the only one I know here. You're the only one who can see me."

"I know and I'm sorry, but it takes too much of my energy." I glanced up when I heard whispering behind me. I needed to get Red out of here and stop talking to open air. *Can you hear me?* I tested.

Red listened intently. "Yeah, I can still hear you."

Then, go back to the cafeteria. I'll stop by after school.

He stared at me for a minute and then stood up abruptly. The chair moved the tiniest bit, but I didn't think anyone noticed. "Fine, I'll go back to my place and wait for you."

I'm sorry.

"Don't waste your pity on me. I'll be fine." He turned on his heel and stormed out of the room, passing Kaleb on the way out. Kaleb shivered and walked over to the table, pushing out the chair Red vacated a moment before.

"Morning," he said, settling his bulk into the chair and scooting it up to the table.

"Hey." I yawned.

"Late night?"

"Something like that." I opened my book as Mr. Clark walked into the room.

Kaleb turned his ice blue eyes to me. They were in stark contrast to his dark skin. "You still up for helping me with my paper tonight?"

Mental head slap. I totally forgot. "Um, sure. Want to come over around seven?"

"Sure."

"I can give you directions."

Kaleb chuckled. It was a nice sound, deep and resonating in his chest. "You forget I live in this town? Everyone knows where everyone lives. I'll be there at seven. Will Evie be there?"

"Um, yeah." I was going to say more, but Mr. Clark cleared his throat and launched into the lesson. I tried to focus, but found my mind wandering back over and over again to Red. *Why was he here? Before I touched him, had he been happy?* Then I sat up straighter. *Maybe that was it. Maybe the spirits relived their happiest memory or their worst memory.* I pressed my lips together. *No, that doesn't make sense either. If they relived their worst memory, they'd be an imprint and reliving their death over and over again. But, if they were -*

Mr. Clark walked by and rapped the table with his knuckles, kicking me out of my thoughts. I looked up and tried to concentrate on what he was saying.

Why were my grandparents reliving a random breakfast repeatedly? Surely that wasn't their happiest memory. What would happen if I touched my grandma like I had touched Red? Would she suddenly wake up and realize she was dead, too? Would that throw her into her worst memory?

I clenched my eyes closed. I felt so guilty about everything I'd done. I'd have to be more careful so I didn't make anything worse. The bell rang and I glanced up at the clock. *One class down, six to go,* I thought, reaching for my bag.

"See you tonight," Kaleb said, holding the door open for me as I walked through.

"Yeah, see you," I responded absently as Andy came out of the crowd and took my elbow in his hand.

"Hey, Anderson," he said, directing me through the hallway.

I jerked my elbow from his grasp. "What are you doing?" I hissed.

"Getting you through your day without having you pass out at some random time. Geez, a little gratefulness would be appreciated."

I rolled my eyes. "I'm fine."

"Of course you are. Now, shut up and let's go. I have to get you to class before I'm late to mine."

The rest of the morning went about the same. I avoided the cafeteria at lunchtime and Evie brought me a sandwich and bottle of water in the art room.

"I think we know where Melanie is," I said around a mouthful of sandwich. Washing it down with water, I cleared my throat. "My grandfather used to be friends with Daniel, um, Red, in high school and after he died, he and my grandma used to play bridge with Melanie and her husband."

"She got married? To someone else?" Tristan asked. His eyebrows rose. "How could she have done that?"

"I think that's what we have to figure out before we try to contact her and get her here," I said. "I mean if she never loved him, then it might be best to leave things alone and try to help Red in some other way."

"But, if she did love him…" Tristan let the idea hang in the air.

"Is she still married?" Andy asked.

I shrugged. "I don't know. Dad said that he thinks she lives in the gold house near the edge of town. We could go over and talk to her after school."

Evie tossed me a look.

"*Before* we go to the courthouse."

Andy and Tristan looked up at me.

I held up my hands. "We're only going to stop by and see if I can get a reading on Sam's spirit. You know, see if any part of him is still there."

Andy shook his head. "No way. Not happening."

"What are you going to do to stop me?" I raised an eyebrow.

"Well, for starters, I'll march you out to see Red and then you'll be too tired to go anywhere after school."

I glared at him, and then remembered my promise. I turned to Evie. "I did promise Red that I'd go see him after school."

"You can't. You won't have enough energy left to reach out to Sam."

"You don't know that. I'll be fine."

Tristan sighed deeply, the sound echoing in the quiet room. "Marissa, we will go with you this afternoon and make sure you don't use too much energy seeing Red. Then, we will go with you to Melanie's house. And, *then,* we'll go with you to the courthouse to look for Sam."

"Great. I'll have my own entourage."

Tristan stood up. "I think that covers all of our bases. Evie, you're taking her to her next class?"

Evie nodded.

"Fine. I'll see you guys later."

"What's up with him?" I asked Andy after Tristan left the room.

"His dad made him apply to Stanford."

"Oh."

I looked at Andy, trying to gauge his feelings. He stuffed a huge bite of burger into his mouth.

I swallowed. "I'm sorry?"

He smiled at me around the bite. "It's fine. I told him that he needs to go. We'll be fine." He stood up and threw his backpack over his shoulder. "Look how well you and Grant are doing."

It's only been a few days.

"Come on, St. Louis. Let's get you to class."

CHAPTER 9

As soon as the last bell rang, I exited my class and found the group waiting for me in the hallway.

"Cafeteria?" Andy asked.

I followed them as they wound their way through the hallways and down the stairs. The cafeteria was quiet and all of the tables and chairs had been broken down and stacked against the walls. The custodian left the wet floor signs up and I skirted around one to get to the outside door. Red was sitting on the tabletop, staring blankly at the bank of windows. Guilt washed over me.

"Hey," I said, sitting down on the table next to him.

"Hi," he said back, not moving his gaze.

Evie, Andy, and Tristan settled onto the bench.

"Your friends are here."

"Yes, Andy, Tristan, and Evie. We can't stay long. We're going to try to find a way to help you this afternoon."

Red turned his eyes to me. I tried to avoid looking at the place where his head was missing.

"How are you going to help me?"

"I don't want to say anything yet, in case it doesn't work." I wrapped my coat around me. "Red, can you trust me?"

He regarded me for a long minute, and then turned back to the school. "I don't really have a choice, do I?"

I squinted and stared down at his feet. A small wisp of dark smoke moved around them, dodging in and out between his ankles. I nodded at Evie and stood up.

"Bye, Red. We'll see you tomorrow." *I hope it's not too late.*

We headed back through the doors and out to the parking lot, none of us saying a word. Evie got into the driver's side of my car and Andy and Tristan followed in his truck. We drove into town, me closing my eyes as we drew nearer. I felt the car stop and dared a glance out through half-closed lids. We were parked on the street in front of a gold house with green shutters.

Evie turned to me. "You stay here. I'm going to see if anyone's home."

"Okay."

"Do you see anyone around here that, um, shouldn't be?"

I opened my eyes wider and turned in my seat as Andy's truck pulled up behind. "Not really, except that guy shoveling his driveway over there." I pointed.

Evie gave me a strange look as she looked in that direction. "I don't see anyone."

"Never mind," I said as the guy grabbed his chest and collapsed. His hat tumbled off his white hair as the shovel fell with a clang on the concrete next to him.

"Close your eyes and wait here," she said, reaching out to pat me on the arm.

I closed my eyes and pushed my chin down into the warmth of my coat. *I hate this! I hate having to be led around everywhere. I hate seeing people dying. I hate it!* I sat there feeling sorry for myself and waiting for Evie to return.

I jumped when the car door opened. A blast of cold air whipped in before she got the door closed behind her and I shivered.

"Sorry," she mumbled and kicked up the heat a notch.

It blew hard on my feet. "What did you find out?" I asked, keeping my eyes closed as I turned the vent toward me.

"She wasn't home."

"Figures."

"We did find something out, though." Evie put the car in gear and started driving.

"What?"

"Her last name. The door had a wreath on it that said, The Ingalls."

"Are we going to the courthouse now?" I asked.

Her silence told me my answer.

It only took about five minutes until the car stopped again. This time, I chanced opening my eyes and I was bombarded with the sight of people everywhere. I sucked in a breath.

"It's four thirty in the afternoon in the middle of town. There are a lot of people here," Evie said quietly.

"Yeah, but how many of them are really here?" I asked, my voice trembling. Already, I felt an enormous amount of energy leaving my body. "We'd better hurry before I pass out," I said, opening my door and hauling my butt out of the seat. I stood looking up at the courthouse. The last time we'd been here, we had navigated through a cave to get to the basement of the behemoth building where I faced something that scared me to death. My heart hurt with the memory of Sam walking into that dark mass. The pain on his face felt real to me all over again as I replayed the scene in my head. Then, Evie was beside me, her hand on my arm.

"You ready?" she asked, her eyes full of hope.

Andy and Tristan walked up and nodded at me.

I drew in a deep breath. "Yeah, I'm ready."

Putting one foot in front of the other, I made my way up the concrete steps that led to the front porch. Evie's grip on my arm tightened as we got closer. At the porch, I could feel the sadness overwhelm me. A mixture of nausea and anger welled up inside me and I balked at the front doors.

"I can't go in there." My voice was practically a whine.

"Why not?" Evie's eyes registered hurt and then understanding. "Oh my gosh," she breathed. "You're surrounded in a blackish brown color." Her free hand flew up to her mouth. "It's awful."

I choked down the bile that rose in my throat and pulled on her arm. "Please, Evie," I said.

"It's okay, St. Louis." She let go of my arm. "I have to go, though. You understand that, right?"

I sank back into Tristan's arms.

"I'll get her back to the car," he said. "You two go in and see if you can find anything."

"Hold on!" Andy sprinted back to his truck and came back with his huge backpack hanging from his shoulder. "We might not need her to find out if Sam's in there." He glanced at me. "Sorry, Anderson."

"It's fine," I said, pulling a breath of fresh air into my lungs. Now that I stepped away from the courthouse, my body was calming down and I felt like myself again. "Evie, how's the color?"

She looked me up and down. "Still looks like a bruise, but there's more of *you* coming through now."

I sighed.

Andy rummaged in his bag and pulled out the phone and speaker he had used at Kristen's house.

"This is the spirit box I made. If we can get close enough, I might be able to talk to Sam." His eyes blazed with excitement. "I mean, if he's here anyway."

"I can try it again," I offered, the sickness in my stomach whirling around as I spoke the words.

Evie shook her head. "I don't think you could go in there even if you wanted to. It's okay. Give Andy and me a couple of minutes."

Andy yanked the huge door open and I blinked hard. In the dimness beyond, I thought I saw a figure standing in the hallway. It looked like Sam for a moment and then I watched as a black tendril of smoke curled out from the figure. It turned this way and that and then seemed to point at me. It headed toward me like a laser, moving fast. I had just enough time to put my hands up in front of my face before the door closed and the smoke was gone.

"Are you okay?" Tristan asked.

I swallowed and glanced once more at the doorway. "Um, yeah. I thought I saw something. Can you take me back to my car now?"

"Sure, of course." He wrapped an arm around my waist and half-carried me along to the car.

I tried the door. "Crap, Evie has the keys."

"Here, come sit in Andy's truck." Tristan hit the key fob in his pocket. The horn honked and the hazards flashed. He helped me up into the cab and then walked around the front of the truck and got in. He turned on the heat and then the headlamps, bathing the front lawn of the courthouse in light.

I looked out into the beams as they cut through the gathering darkness. People moved along, in and out of the light, their faces somehow familiar and forgotten all at once. I closed my eyes. "Please turn them off."

Tristan furrowed his brow at me and cut the headlamps. "Seriously, Marissa, are you okay? What happened back there?"

I shook my head and rubbed my hand across my forehead. "I don't know. It's like whatever awful thing is in the basement, is affecting me even more. It used to only happen when I was close to the basement door, you know, in that hallway, but now it's worse, and I wasn't even as close."

"Maybe it got stronger when it took Sam."

I looked over at Tristan. He was staring out the windshield at the building on the hill.

"I thought that, too." I pulled my knees up to my chest and chewed on my thumbnail. After a minute of silence, I cleared my throat. "I thought I saw Sam."

Tristan turned to look at me. "When?"

"Before."

He raised his eyebrows.

"I thought I saw him this morning in my bathroom. The room got really cold and I thought I saw him standing behind me in the shower. Then, when Andy and Evie went into the courthouse just now, I thought I saw him standing there in the hallway. A tendril of black mist started to come at me before they closed the door."

Tristan already had his phone out texting. He watched the screen for a moment and then hit the steering wheel. "He's not answering. Why didn't you tell me that before you let them walk in there?"

I winced at the tone of his words and at my own stupidity. "It can't hurt them," I said in a small voice. "Right?"

"Wait here," Tristan said. He opened the door and jumped down. "And lock the doors." Slamming it closed behind him, he ran up the concrete steps and disappeared into the building.

I squinted, trying to watch for any movement.

Suddenly, a loud thump from the side of the truck sounded. I looked over and saw a face staring at me through the window. It was a man, his chapped lips pulled back from his rotting teeth and his eyes rolling wildly in their sockets.

"Hey! You got a hit? I need a hit!" He glared at me, his hair falling in dirty strings from under his filthy cap. "Hey! You can see me, can't you?"

I stared at him, my breath caught in my throat. Closing my eyes, I tried to tell myself that he wasn't there. No one was really there. Then, I heard another thump. This time, it was from the driver's door. I opened my eyes and saw another man.

A huge, overweight man, his face held the sheen of sweat on it. He was wearing a suit and the front of it was covered in vomit. He held onto his neck as he stared through the window at me.

"Do you know the Heimlich? I've got something stuck in my throat," he croaked at me.

Through the windshield, I saw several people walking my way. One lady was covered in animal bites and was bleeding from a gash in her neck. Her eyes were open and vacant. A boy made his way slowly to the truck, his body mangled and a tire track running down his shirt.

Whimpers escaped my lips as I fumbled for my phone in my pocket. The voices outside the truck were demanding, insistent and I could feel the frustration and sadness coming off them. Tears fell as I texted Evie. *Help!*

I reached over and locked the doors, putting my head down onto my knees and squeezing my eyes shut. Their voices cut through the windows.

"Hey! Help me! I need a hit!"

"Where's my mommy?"

"I asked if I could pet her dog."

"It feels like I'm going to choke."

Go away. Stop. I can't help you all!

I rocked back and forth on the seat, covering my ears and crying. Then, a moment later, I felt every last bit of energy being pulled from my body as I let go, allowing sleep to take me.

Chapter 10

"I'm so tired of this."

Those were my first words when I came to in Andy's truck. It was almost dark and we were on the highway. The dashboard lights lit up Andy's face as he drove.

He glanced over at me. "You and me both, Anderson."

I sat up and adjusted the seatbelt to fit more comfortably now that I was upright. The view outside the windows told me that we were almost to my house.

"Where's Tristan?"

Andy's eyes flitted up to the rearview. "They're right behind me in your car."

"Can I have a drink?" I grabbed his soda from the center console and didn't wait for an answer as I gulped it down, letting the sweetness coat my throat and the caffeine begin to work on my exhaustion.

"Um, sure. I didn't buy it for myself or anything." He paused. "But now I see that you obviously need it more than I do and you should probably just keep it for yourself."

He said all of this while I was still drinking, and when I finally tipped the bottle from my lips, I hiccupped and then burped.

"It's definitely yours now."

I chuckled. "Thanks."

He tossed a worried glance my way.

I bristled. "Quit looking at me like that."

"You have no idea, do you?"

"About what?" I placed the bottle in the console and crossed my arms over my chest.

He looked over at me again. "How bad you scared us tonight."

I felt the curve in the road before I saw it. "Hey, can you pull over here?"

"Where?"

I pointed to the shoulder. "Just up here."

Andy slowed and turned on his blinker, then his hazards. I unbuckled and was out of the truck before it fully stopped. My car pulled off the road behind Andy's and Evie rolled down her window.

"Get back in the truck, St. Louis."

I ignored her and checked for traffic both ways before I sprinted across the pavement. I got to the edge of the road and looked down. Below was the same car I'd seen the day before. The same woman was running around, banging on the window and screaming for help.

I heard a car door shut behind me and then several footsteps as my friends crossed the road.

"What are you doing? You don't have the energy for this," Tristan said.

"I'm fine. I just have to check something." I slid down the embankment, partly on my feet and partly on my rear end in the snow. Standing up, I brushed the snow from me and walked around the car. "Evie! Come here!"

A moment later, Evie was next to me.

"Can you see anything around them?"

Evie took a deep breath, closed her eyes, and then opened them again. She concentrated on the area in front of us. "I-I, um, I still don't see anything here."

I stared at the woman's feet and tilted my head. A white wisp rose around her, bathing her in a smoky shield.

"Beth?" I said quietly.

The woman continued to scream and try to rouse her husband from his place ensconced in the car. I moved closer.

"My name is Marissa and this is Evie. We want to try to help you, okay?" I felt my insides shaking. *Is this the right thing to do?* I shook my head, trying to shake away the voice of negativity. *It should work the opposite that it did for Red. Since I took him out of a good memory, I screwed things up. If I can take her out of this bad memory, I can help her move on.* I reached out and touched the woman on the shoulder. Electricity moved between us and I drew my hand back when I felt the exchange lessen.

"Beth?" I breathed.

Her eyes turned slowly to me and then her body. She shifted and she was now in a hospital gown, her stomach distended under the folds of the gown. She reached down, touched her stomach, and then looked up at me with her mouth open.

"What's happening?" Evie hissed in my ear.

"She's still here, but she's different."

"How?"

Beth gazed at me a moment more and then turned her face upward toward the heavens.

"She's looking up. Oh, Evie, I think she's moving on!"

Beth spread her arms and threw her head back, a look of pure joy on her face. She closed her eyes and a bright light spread around us with a sonic boom.

"Can you see this, Evie?" I whispered. I turned to look at Evie and it took me a minute to register the expression on her face. It wasn't happiness, rather, it was sadness and horror. "Wait, what's wrong?"

"There's a disturbance now. It's flowing up, pushing against the fabric in a spike."

"No!" I whipped around to watch Beth. "She's better now."

Beth raised up off the ground for a moment, her entire body bathed in a beautiful, gentle light and then she stopped. Her body jerked as if it was being pulled by something.

"No, no, no," I whispered, tilting my head and squinting. Where the white mist had been before, a snake of black smoke filled in. I followed its path up to Beth's ankle, where it wrapped around, caressing her ankle and urging her back from her upward journey.

She sucked in a huge breath and then looked down at the car. Anguish rushed over her features, distorting them. She let out a cry and the light around us faded as she turned, her arms now outstretched toward the car, toward her Brandon.

"No! Keep going!" I shouted, rushing forward and throwing myself on the ground near the place from which the smoke emanated. I grabbed at it, swiping it away, pulling at it, but it escaped my hands. It blew away, but snapped back as soon as my hand moved, its relentless pull on Beth not abating. "Let her go!" I shouted.

Beth's bare feet alit near me in the snow and she crouched down near the car. She peered through the driver's side window and hit it again and again, crying out over and over for her Brandon.

Tears ran down my face as I watched.

Andy's hands were on my shoulders. "Come on, Anderson. Let's get you back into the car."

"I can't leave! I messed everything up again!" I clawed at my chest, trying to remove the overwhelming pressure of the guilt. "She was leaving, Andy! She was going but something was holding her here! I can't get rid of it!" I swiped again at the smoke and my hand came away frozen. I cried out with the pain and held my hand to me.

"Andy, we have to get her out of here. Now!" Evie's voice was scared.

I stood up and yanked my arm from their grasp. "No! I am not leaving another mess that I created. Look at her," I swept my uninjured hand behind me. "I can't leave her."

Beth continued to scream and cry, banging her hands against the window.

I turned and knelt in the snow beside her. "Beth, can you hear me?"

She stopped for a moment and turned her eyes to me. They were filled with tears.

"I remember it all now," she said. "I remember the accident and I remember trying to get Brandon out of the car. They took me to the hospital and they tried to fix me. The doctors told me that Brandon was going to be okay. He was going to be fine." She stared at the car, tears sliding silently down her cheeks. "He's not fine." Her face broke as she let out a scream that echoed into the night.

"Anderson, we have to go. The sheriff is here."

I looked up and saw the blue and red lights reflecting off the treetops that I could see from the ditch.

"Why did you show me this?" Beth asked in a small voice.

"I-I'm sorry," I said. "I was trying to help." I felt pressure on my arms as Evie and Andy pulled on me.

Beth's eyes followed me as my friends led me up the embankment. Her gaze silently asked *why* over and over again into the night. Then, I was on the side of the road, trying to stand upright when all I wanted to do was go to sleep.

Andy's voice came through muffled. "...wanted to see where they died. I know it was stupid, officer. Yes, sir. She's fine. Twisted her ankle on the way down. We're headed home right now."

They led me to Andy's truck and shoved me into the passenger seat. I buckled up and sat with my head in my hands. Andy got in and turned on the truck. He waited for the sheriff to leave before he pulled out onto the road.

"I'm so sorry," I said between my fingers. "I don't know what I was thinking."

Andy's lips were drawn in a thin line. We were almost to my driveway before he finally spoke.

"Well, we've seen how your way works. You think we could try being a team again now?"

CHAPTER 11

"What happened when I left the truck?" Tristan sat on my futon, his white tennis shoes blazing in the overhead light.

I never knew how he kept them so white even in the winter. I shook my head to clear it.

"Uh, sorry. What?"

He repeated the question and I told the group what I saw at the courthouse.

Andy leaned over the back of my office chair, his chin resting on his hands. "We came running when we got your message. Evie said she saw a huge disturbance over the truck and colors were shooting out of you right through the roof of the cab."

"It was really strange, St. Louis."

"Sorry, I didn't mean to worry you all."

"Don't be sorry!" Evie leaned over and placed her hand on my arm. The springs on my bed squeaked as she sat up straight again. "Whatever's going on, you are, like, a *beacon* now for these spirits."

"Only the sad ones," I mumbled.

"You're on to something there," Andy said. "I think when you went down into the courthouse basement, you were exposed to something really bad."

"And really good," I said.

"Well, whatever you were exposed to ripped the veil right off the second layer."

"The second world?" Evie asked.

Andy shrugged. "We're one layer, ghosts are another."

"Are there more?" I asked. "Layers, I mean."

Tristan sat up, tenting his fingers as his elbow rested on his knees. "There are several theories out there that profess that there are several layers of consciousness."

"Preach," Andy said.

I ignored him. "So, I'm able to see both, all the time?"

Tristan nodded.

"How do I get it to stop?"

"We could go back to the basement of the courthouse."

Coldness washed through me and fear made my eyes water.

"We might have to do it anyway," Evie said.

"Um, why?"

Andy cleared his throat. "When we went into the building, we made it to the back corner, you know, by the basement door. I set up the spirit box and we were able to hear something before Tristan came in to get us."

"What?" I found myself leaning up over my knees. "What did you hear?"

"Marissa?" My dad's voice followed a knock on my door.

"Yeah?"

He opened the door and his eyes scanned over the people in my room before focusing on me. "There's a boy downstairs who said he was here to work on a paper with you?"

"Oh, man! I totally forgot." I stood up.

"We have to get going anyway." Andy stood up as well and stretched.

"Hold on." I looked at Dad. "Can you give us a couple more minutes?"

Dad pressed his lips together.

I held up two fingers. "Two minutes. Please? His name's Kaleb. He's a football player. Can't you talk about running meters or tackling the defensive start?"

Dad held up his hand. "Stop. Just stop." He smiled and closed the door behind him as he left.

I whirled around. "What did you hear?"

"We heard Sam. Or, at least, we think it was him."

"What was he saying?" I asked, rubbing my arms as goosebumps rose up along them.

Evie and Andy exchanged a look. "He was calling out for his daughter, Sarah."

I closed my eyes and took a deep breath. "Okay, here's what we're going to do. Tonight, I am going to help Kaleb write his paper so that he doesn't fail English Comp and have to drop out of football and turn to a life of crime. Tomorrow, after school, we're going to track down Melanie and try to get her in to meet with Red. Then, we're going to come back here and gather our equipment. We're going to go to Kristen's house and find out what's going on there. And then, Saturday, we're going to go back into the courthouse basement to confront whatever's there and make it give up Sam."

My speech was met with silence.

Finally, Evie spoke. "Um, that sounds pretty solid."

The plan was set in place. Evie took Andy and Tristan down the back stairs to let them out and I headed down the front stairs to the living room. Kaleb sat on the couch, his bulk weighing down cushions in the middle. He stood up as soon as I came down the stairs.

"Hey, Marissa."

"Hey."

"Kaleb and I have been talking about defensive tackles and home runs." Dad kicked the footrest down on his recliner and walked past me to his office.

"Nice to meet you, Mr. Anderson." Kaleb said. Then he turned to me. "Thanks for agreeing to do this tonight. I really do appreciate it."

"No worries," I said absently. I sat down on the couch and pulled my laptop from the armrest. "Let's see this paper."

Kaleb stared at the opening at the back of the living room that led into the dining room.

"Um, hi," he said.

I turned to see who he was talking to.

Evie stood in the kitchen door, her hair pulled up on top of her head and a huge sweatshirt hanging down to her knees. She held a soda in one hand and was taking a bite out of a snack cake with her other.

"Hi," she said with her mouth full. She raised her eyebrows. "Have fun with that paper."

"Oh, uh, you could stay down here while we work," Kaleb said. "I don't mind." His eyes never wavered from her as a tentative smile spread across his face.

Oh my gosh. He likes her!

"No, thanks. I have a date with a bubble bath tonight."

She disappeared up the stairs and Kaleb stood staring at the place she vacated.

"Kaleb?"

He turned and smiled at me. "Yeah. Paper." He glanced once more at the kitchen and then sat down and pulled his binder from his bag.

We worked together on his paper and a couple hours later, it resembled something that would be in the ballpark of a passing grade. I let him out and then said goodnight to my dad before climbing the stairs to my room. A strip of light under Evie's door told me that she was awake. I knocked softly.

"Come in."

I opened the door. Evie sat on her bed, wet black ringlets of hair framing her face.

"Hey, are you okay?"

She furrowed her brow. "Why wouldn't I be?"

"I mean about Sam."

She shrugged then smiled. "He's still there, St. Louis. I mean, that's all I can ask for, right? We'll get him out of there." She said it with such confidence that I swallowed my doubts.

"Sure we will. Night."

"Night."

I couldn't sleep, so I sat up for hours, listening to the wind whip the tree branches outside my window. Finally, I gave up on sleep and wandered down to the kitchen. I sat at the table and watched my grandparents cycle through their breakfast twice before I felt so drained I could hardly make it up the stairs again.

I fell into bed and into a dreamless sleep.

CHAPTER 12

The next afternoon, Evie and I beat it out of school as soon as the last bell rang. We practically ran to my car and headed over to Melanie's house. This time, when we arrived, a late model sedan was parked in the driveway. Evie pulled my car up to the curb across the street and Andy drove up and parked behind us.

"Ready to do this?" Evie's cheeks were full of color.

I tucked my chin into my scarf. The wind blew icy around us and I shoved my hands into my pockets as we climbed the three porch steps and stood outside her front door. Andy rang the doorbell and we waited.

A moment later, a shadow passed in front of the frosted window in the door. Then, the lock clicked and the door opened. A tiny woman with gray hair pulled into a low bun stood at the screen door.

"Hi, Mrs. Ingalls, my name is Marissa and this is Andy, Tristan, and Evie."

"Good afternoon. I actually have someone that takes care of shoveling my driveway, but thank you anyway," she said and started to close the door.

"My dad is John Anderson," I blurted out.

The door stopped and she peered at me with cautious eyes. "Johnny?" A whisper of a smile passed on her face and then sadness took its place. She pushed open her screen door. "Come on in."

I looked over at Evie. She raised her eyebrows and then followed me into the house. Once inside, Tristan closed the door behind him and we all stood cramped in the front foyer. It opened up to a neat living room that held a floral couch with matching wingback chairs near the window. Two huge curios flanked the ancient television set and the orange shag carpeting was worn down in a path from the chair to the kitchen beyond. Mrs. Ingalls stood with her back to us, running water in a tea kettle at the sink. An old man sat nodding off in one of the chairs and I raised my hand in greeting.

"Hi, Mr. Ingalls..." My voice faded as Evie placed a hand on my arm. She shook her head.

Oh, he's a ghost.

"Put your things on the coat rack and have a seat. I'll have some hot tea ready in just a minute," Mrs. Ingalls called from the kitchen.

There was a flurry of activity in the foyer as we all unwrapped from our coats, hats, gloves, and scarves. Then, another flurry of activity and whispered directions of where to sit. Andy almost sat on Mr. Ingalls before I motioned madly to him to join us on the couch. We sat, side by side, sandwiched on the floral couch until Evie finally rolled her eyes, pulled out the bench at the piano, and sat down on it. Andy, Tristan, and I readjusted and spread out on the cushions.

Mrs. Ingalls brought in a tray with steaming cups of tea and some butter cookies. She placed them on the coffee table in front of us and then groaned as she sat down in the chair nearest us. I noticed that she glanced at the chair next to her before she did so. She caught me looking and smiled.

"He's been gone six years now, and I still check his chair to make sure he's not asleep and missing his show."

Andy and Evie launched themselves into the cookies and I could hear them crunching to the beat of the seconds ticking away on the giant grandfather clock in the quiet living room. I shook my head to clear it and took a sip of the hot tea. I usually preferred hot chocolate, but this was delicious; sweet and hot with a hint of peppermint. I took another sip and then placed the cup back onto the table.

"Thank you for the tea and snacks, Mrs. Ingalls."

"Call me Melanie. Mrs. Ingalls makes me feel old."

I smiled. "Sure."

"So, you're Johnny's daughter, huh?" Her eyes appraised me. "You look just like him."

"Yes, ma'am."

She brought the teacup to her lips and took a small sip. "I heard he moved back to town a few months ago. I wasn't surprised that he hasn't come to see me after..." she glanced up at me. "How do you like Culvers Grove so far?"

Oh, besides the fact that it's absolutely filled with ghosts? I smiled again. "Um, it's different than St. Louis."

"I was sure sorry to hear about your mother. We all were."

"Thank you, we're adjusting." It was the pat answer I gave anytime someone I didn't know expressed sympathy over my mom dying. It felt like a dance that I had done before. "Melanie, we're here because we met someone that knew you a long time ago."

She chuckled, the wrinkles running from the corners of her eyes deepening with the action. "That wouldn't be hard to do in a town this small. Throw a rock and you'll hit someone that knows me."

Andy leaned up and grabbed another cookie. "Do you know a Daniel Trenton?"

The color drained from Melanie's face and her denim blue eyes grew suddenly guarded. "How did you all hear about Daniel?" She turned her gaze to me. "Did your father tell you about him?"

I cleared my throat. "He only said that he remembered his father hanging out with Daniel in high school. He was a football star and he signed up for the armed forces as soon as he turned eighteen." I lowered my voice. "He also told me that you and Daniel were supposed to get engaged before he left for Vietnam."

She brought a tissue out from the wrist of her sweater and dabbed at her eyes. "He never made it home."

"We're very sorry," Evie said from her perch on the bench.

Melanie dabbed again at her eyes. "That was a number of years ago. A whole other lifetime." She swept a hand at the pictures that filled the curios and sat on top of the television. "I got married and had a son, and then lost a son and then a husband. Did your dad tell you about Thomas?" The name hung in the air, carried along the space between us with gossamer wings of anguish. It flitted toward me and my eyes filled with tears.

I shook my head. "Only that they used to play together when you and my grandparents played bridge and that he died in an accident."

Melanie grunted and stood up, giving her legs a moment to stop shaking before she moved across the living room to the television set. She plucked a picture frame from the top and gazed down at it before brushing the dust from the glass with a withered dry hand. She came back to the chair and sat down, then handed the picture to me.

I took it and stared down at the photograph that had grown faded with age. In it, a younger version of my dad stood next to an old car in the driveway of the house we were sitting in at this moment. I smiled. My dad was shirtless, his skinny frame leaned against the side of the car, his foot on the running board. He wore jean cutoffs, sunglasses and a bandana was tied around his long hair. Another young man stood near the front of the car in a white shirt and a pair of jeans.

"That was the day they bought that old thing. They were going to restore it to its former glory." Melanie's eyes sparkled. "That was the happiest I ever saw those two."

"Thank you for showing it to me," I said, passing the picture over to Tristan and Andy. Evie leaned over to look, too.

"It was three months later that Thomas died."

Emotion hit me in the gut. I felt hot tears well in my eyes again. "C-can I ask what happened?"

Melanie regarded me from the chair that nearly swallowed her small frame. She took another sip of tea and nodded to herself. "I think you need to ask your dad about that. It's not my place."

Tristan passed the picture back to me and I handed it to Melanie.

She took it from me and held it reverently in her lap, looking down at it once more.

"Thank you," I said. *Why doesn't she want to talk about it?* Then, *what's Dad keeping from me?*

Melanie placed the cup back on its saucer and put it on the table. "Now, you must have had a reason to come calling on an old lady on a Friday afternoon."

I looked over at Evie. She smiled at me.

"Ma'am, I'm not sure how to tell you this, but Daniel, um, Red, is still at school." I took a deep breath and plunged on. "He was sitting on the picnic table outside the cafeteria and I went out to talk to him. He said he was waiting there to ask Melanie to marry him."

Melanie's hand flew up to her mouth and she gasped.

I sat up on the edge of the couch and reached over to lay my hand on hers. "Are you okay?"

She nodded quickly, her teary eyes wide beyond the tissue she held to her mouth.

"I, um, I talked to him and he said that he was waiting to ask you to marry him, and then I touched him and he, um, remembered things."

"Like what?" The question was shaky, but her gaze was strong.

I continued. "He said he remembered shipping out to basic training and feeling so alone. And how he had to go to Vietnam and how while he was on a mission, he was killed." I patted her hand. "He doesn't remember asking you to marry him. He can't remember that part. He doesn't know what you would have said and he's all alone there and so sad, and..." I took another deep breath, not sure what else to say and waiting for Melanie to tell us to leave.

Instead, she tucked the tissue back into her sleeve and stood up. She looked at me. "You remind me so much of your father. I wish now I would have..." She trailed off and began placing our cups back on the tray. She wiped up the crumbs in front of Andy with a deft hand.

"I'm sorry, Mrs. Ingalls, we, um," I glanced over at Evie for help.

Melanie held a weathered hand up. "I suggest you all get your coats on so we can get over there." Then, she took the tray and carried it to the kitchen.

I looked over at the group and they looked back at me.

Melanie swept back into the living room. "Well?"

"Y-yes, ma'am."

We stood up, gathered our coats, and bundled up.

Melanie pulled on a huge pea green wool coat and jammed a fuzzy white hat on top of her head. It sat there askew as she pulled on a pair of magenta gloves and grabbed her pocketbook from the shelf of the closet. Her eyes sparkled and her cheeks were red.

She cocked an eyebrow. "Do either of you ladies have any lipstick?"

CHAPTER 13

I sat in the backseat of my car, Evie's and my backpacks on the seat next to me. Melanie was buckled into the passenger seat, the sunshade pulled down, applying a coating of Evie's plum colored lipstick to her wrinkled lips. The car bumped and she tossed a glance over to Evie.

"Sorry," she mumbled.

I turned to make sure Andy's truck was behind us as we turned into the school parking lot. Only a few cars were left in the lot.

"Is there anything going on at school tonight?" I asked.

"No, there's Mr. J's car and the rest are teachers, I think."

"Pull behind the school over there." I pointed to the drive that led behind the gym wing.

Evie pulled the car up near a set of trailers in the back and Andy pulled in next to her. The vehicles would be hidden to anyone looking outside the school and the blinds in the trailer were drawn.

"Are you ready?" I asked Melanie.

She narrowed her eyes, her jaw set. "Yes, I am."

We all piled out and stood by the corner of the trailer.

"Let's go this way," Andy said. He led the way to the far side of the trailer and then around the brick end of the building. We ducked beneath the windows of the lower set of classrooms. It was only four o'clock, but the wind carried the icy edge of nighttime on it.

At the corner of the cafeteria, Tristan leaned out to look in the windows. "No one's there," he said. "Come on."

We moved around the corner and into the quiet place outside the doors with the picnic table. Red sat on the table, his back to us as he placed a rock on the table. He turned when he heard us approach and jumped down off the table.

"I didn't think you were coming back," he said.

Hi, Red.

His eyes scanned over the group. "Someone else is with you." His voice grew guarded and he took a step back.

We found Melanie.

Red's face broke. A million emotions ran in quick succession over his features. Then, he spoke. His tone was quiet, hopeful. "Melanie?" The way he said it, his voice practically caressed her name.

She's here, Red. She's here. I turned to Melanie. "He's standing in front of the picnic table."

She smiled and looked hopefully in the direction I was looking. She leaned in to me. "I can't see him," she whispered.

"Here." I took off my glove and held my hand out. Melanie followed suit and placed her warm hand in mine. I turned to the group. "I'm going to let them talk to each other, okay?"

Andy nodded. "We've got your back, Anderson."

"Come on," I said, leading Melanie gently toward Red. *Can you see her yet?*

Red squinted. He shook his head. "I can see you, but not her."

I glanced down at his feet. The black mist gathered, stronger now. *You have to shake off the mist.*

He followed my gaze and then looked back up at me, panic in his eyes. "What is that?"

It's something bad. You have to pull away from it, Red. Okay?

He closed his eyes, concentrating.

I thought I saw the mist waver a bit, but then it latched on again. It led from his feet to the table. On the top was a half circle of rocks and the mist disappeared into the center of it. *What is that?*

He swept at the rocks, but they only shuddered a bit.

Melanie took a sharp breath in. "Did you see that?" she whispered.

"It's okay, Melanie. Andy? Can you come push these rocks off the table?"

Red shook his head. "I'm sorry. I thought it was the only way."

For what?

His voice wavered. "To make it all go away. A man came to me and said that I could build a circle and it would make all of the pain go away. I could move on through the circle."

I felt my heart thump in my chest. *Red, what did the man look like?*

Red's eyes darted around as Andy moved forward toward the table. "I don't know. He was about my age and had a hat on."

Did he tell you his name? A bad feeling began to wind its way up through my middle. *Red? Did he?*

He shook his head. "No, I'm sorry."

It's okay. "Andy?"

Andy took a hand and pushed the rocks away. When he did, the black mist was cut off completely. The connection between the table and Red was severed and the mist swirled angrily at his feet before fading.

I swallowed. *Give me your hand.*

Red brushed his hand on the leg of his pants and held it out to me. I squeezed my hand tighter on Melanie's and then reached out and took Red's. Electricity wound its way up and through me and I threw my head back, gritting my teeth against the sensation and the draining feeling. I dared to take a look at Melanie and drew a breath in through my teeth. She was young again, with long, brown straight hair, a flowered headband holding her hair back from her face. Her eyes were bright and happy and her skin was flawless. Red looked exactly like the day I first saw him. He wore a uniform that was clean and pressed and his face was young and happy. He smiled, his features handsome as he stared at his love.

"Melanie," he breathed, "can you hear me?"

She ducked her head and looked up at him through her thick lashes. "I forgot how handsome you were," she said, her face breaking out in a wide smile. "I miss you so much, Daniel."

A tear slipped from his eye and wound its way down his cheek as he stared at her, his eyes roving over her face as if he were drinking in every single feature. "You're so beautiful."

She smiled. "No, I'm an old woman."

"You look just like the day I left."

Her smile faded and she took a deep breath. "Why did you leave without asking me?"

His eyes registered hurt. "I waited right here. I remember now. I came here before leaving for basic training. I wanted to ask you before I left, but you weren't here." His chest rose and fell as he spoke, his voice full of emotion. "I waited for you and you never came. I had to leave."

Melanie began to cry. "I didn't come to school. I thought you'd already left, and I was heartbroken that you left without telling me goodbye."

"Oh, Melanie, I'm so sorry. I talked a buddy of mine into stopping at school to ask you before we went to Fort Leonard Wood. We had to leave. The bus was waiting for us."

"I never knew."

"I wanted you to. I started a hundred letters to you from Vietnam, but I never sent them. I wanted to be a man the next time you saw me. I wanted to be able to offer you something, a better life."

"Any life with you would have been better than a life without," Melanie whispered.

"I am so sorry. I have always loved you."

"And I have always loved you."

He shook his head.

I could feel the energy draining from me and I gritted my teeth, holding on to their hands.

"What can I do?" Red whispered.

Melanie looked up at him, tears running down her face. She smiled the saddest smile I'd ever seen. "Ask me."

He furrowed his brow.

"Ask me now. After all these years, Daniel, ask me to marry you. I want you to know."

He took a deep, shuddering breath and fumbled in the chest pocket of his jacket with his free hand. He pulled out a small box and flipped it open. A small diamond ring caught the setting sun's rays and glinted softly.

"Melanie Ann Turner, would you do me the honor of being my wife?"

Melanie's chin quivered and her voice cracked when she spoke. "Yes, Daniel. My answer would have been yes." She smiled and then pulled her hand from mine. In front of my eyes, she turned into an old woman again, her wrinkled face wet with tears. She smiled and nodded, and then turned and walked back to Evie and Tristan.

Red smiled. His eyes caught mine and he wiped the tear from his cheek. "She said yes."

Yes, she did.

He looked at me and took my hand in both of his. He eyes held mine. "Thank you, Marissa. Thank you so much."

Then, he let go of my hands and the world shifted. As soon as the connection between us was broken, all of the energy ran out of me and I fell to the ground. Andy and Tristan were at my side and they helped me up.

"Is it done?" Tristan asked.

I watched Red for a moment. He was sitting on the picnic table in his uniform, the ring box in his hand. His voice was muted but I heard his words: "Will you marry me, will you marry me, will you marry me?" he muttered. "If she says no, you can pull out the but I'm going off to war card. No one could say no to that."

I squinted and cocked my head. A white mist curled around Red's feet. "Yeah, it's done." My head rolled to the side and rested on Andy's shoulder. I closed my eyes. I felt them begin to walk and I tried to move my feet, but guessed I wasn't being much help on the way to the car.

They helped me into the backseat and Tristan leaned over to buckle me in. "We're going to follow you back to Melanie's house."

I nodded, my head lolling to the side with the effort.

Evie and Melanie got in and Evie started the car. I felt the car moving and I rested my arms on a backpack and my chin on my arms.

"Mrs. Ingalls?"

"Yes, dear."

The voices from the front seat were comforting, like when my parents used to take me on road trips. I would bunk down in the backseat while they talked and laughed together in the front. I felt warm, safe, and tired. So very tired.

"How could you let him go like that? How could you just walk away after all of those years?"

There was a moment of silence and then Melanie's voice.

"Because, dear, that was my past. What good would it do to spend my life, or what little I have of it left anyway, pining away for the love of a memory…a ghost?"

I let my eyes close as the evening closed in.

CHAPTER 14

The car was cold when I came to. I looked around, trying to get my bearings. I was in the backseat of my car and I was alone. It was nearly dark outside the car windows and my breath made a circle of condensation on the inside of the window as I peered out. I pulled my phone from my pocket and touched the screen. The phone sprang to life and the blue light lit up the interior of the car. It was 5:14. I leaned over and looked out the other window. The car was parked on the street in front of Melanie's house and the warm lights from the windows spilled out into the cold night. I shivered, and wrapped my coat around me, imagining my friends toasty warm in Melanie's living room.

I sent a text to Evie. *I'm awake. And cold.*

A moment later, the front door of the house opened and Evie leaned out and held one finger up, and then she disappeared inside again.

I rubbed my eyes, pushing the sleepiness away and stretching the best I could in the constraining backseat. I opened the back door and switched to the front seat as Evie, Tristan, and Andy came out on the front porch. I could hear them saying goodbye and Melanie waved from her door. I raised my hand in response.

"Hey, St. Louis, you're awake." Evie sat down behind the wheel.

"Yeah, thanks for leaving me in the cold."

"Shut up. Here." Evie handed me a huge steaming travel cup. "It's coffee. Strong. She added about a bag and a half of sugar, but it should do the trick."

I took the warm cup gratefully and blew on the opening. The steam spread away from me and I took a sip. The hot liquid tasted like roofing tar and dirt, but I drank as much as I could without burning my tongue. "Mmmm. Thanks."

Evie turned on the car and handed me a napkin wrapped around a huge slice of cake.

I took it and dove in, letting crumbs fall all over the front of my coat as I devoured the cake.

Evie watched me with a look of disgust on her face. "Taking tips from Andy?"

I threw my middle finger up at her and she laughed.

"Let's go home," she said, putting the car in gear.

"Can you still walk through walls?" I asked around a bite of cake.

She glanced over. "No."

"You didn't call me when you tried?"

"It wasn't pretty, but, I can sort of, well, *reach* through some things if I really concentrate."

"Does it bother you?" I polished off the rest of the cake and proceeded to pick the crumbs off my jacket and place them in my mouth.

"Does what bother me?" Evie turned through the maze of small roads on the outskirts of town. I appreciated that she wasn't driving through the center of town even though it would have been the shorter route home. I didn't think I could handle seeing all of those spirits tonight.

"That your powers are going away."

She shrugged and stopped at the stop sign. "I mean, I guess, but I didn't have them for so long that I'm going to miss them."

"You can see disturbances?"

"Yeah."

"And colors around people?"

"Yep."

"And you can sort of reach through things?"

"What are you thinking?"

"I'm going to need you to stop by Beth's on the way home."

She cast a worried glance my way and headed onto the highway. "Why?"

"I have an idea."

"You want to clue me in before we get there, or are you still working this lone wolf angle?"

I jerked my head back. "Lone wolf angle?"

"Yeah, you've been doing all sorts of things all on your own. I thought we were a team."

I took a sip of the coffee. "We are."

"Andy and Tristan don't think so."

"Listen, Andy and I are square, and if Tristan has a problem with how I'm doing things, he's a big boy and he can talk to me."

Evie was quiet.

"See, I think the real problem here is that it's you that has a problem with what I'm doing, and if you do, you should say something."

"Fine. *Something.*"

I snorted. "Clever. What do you have a problem with?"

"I have a problem with the fact that you are running all over the country helping out every ghost you run into. Oh, that random ghost over there? Let's drop everything and help him. That one over there? I've never met her and she means nothing to me, but let's go ahead and help her, too."

"And you think we should be helping a certain ghost in particular?"

She was quiet for a moment. "Yeah, I do. I think he's in trouble, St. Louis."

I took a deep breath. "I *know* he's in trouble. I don't know if he's the same Sam you and I knew a few weeks ago. You don't remember anything about being held by that dark thing?"

Evie shuddered. "Some of it comes back at times."

"It's awful, isn't it?"

Evie nodded, her eyes filling with tears.

"Are you ready to talk about it?"

She shook her head and swiped at her eyes with the back of her gloved hand. She sniffed loudly. "What do you want to do at Beth's? We're almost there."

I swished down another sludgy mouthful of coffee. It was about the grossest thing I'd ever ingested, but it was certainly doing the trick. I felt alert and almost back to my former self.

"So, after Red talked to Melanie tonight, he was able to go back to before I touched him."

"He's still there? I didn't see a disturbance after you let go of Melanie. I thought he'd gone."

I shook my head. "I don't think they can move on. Something's holding them here, so the best I can do is get them back to the happy memory. Back to the point where they don't know that they're a ghost."

"That makes no sense."

"It's not ideal. I mean, I would love to help them move on, but I don't think that's possible right now."

"Okay, so why Beth and why tonight? We have to go to Kristen's. Aren't you pushing your energy a lot?"

"I'll be okay. Remember how I saw a black mist around your dad?" I glanced over. I didn't want to mention her dad.

She didn't seem fazed by the mention. "Yeah, you saw it in the memories and you saw it when he was with me in the hospital."

"Right. Well, when the ghosts are in distress, I can see the same black mist around them."

"What about the ghosts that aren't in distress?"

"A white mist."

"Seriously?"

I kept going with my train of thought. "When I touched Red, the mist around him turned black. He was so sad and distraught and he didn't want to deal with the pain anymore. He was building some sort of circle and he said that someone told him that it would stop the pain."

Evie was quiet for a long time. "And you think Beth might be doing the same thing to get away from her pain."

"Exactly. And if we can stop it, we can help her."

"Like, reset her to before she knew she was dead?"

"Yeah."

"How?" Evie slowed down as we rounded the corner. She turned on her blinker.

"You're going to help me reach through and wake up her husband."

Evie pulled the car over to the shoulder and put it in park. She looked over at me. "You think this will work?"

"We have to try. It's my fault that she's where she's at now."

Evie stared at me for a long time and then got out of the car.

"What the heck, Patton?" Andy's voice carried from behind.

I took one last drink of coffee and then climbed out of the car. I crossed the road and stood at the top of the ditch, looking down at the upside-down car. When I heard my friends behind me, I turned.

"Ready?"

Evie nodded solemnly and followed me down the hill.

"What do you see?" I whispered as we neared the car. Something felt different, wrong.

Evie stopped and concentrated. "I, um, I see a massive disturbance, and the color is all wrong here."

"Okay." I took a step forward and then said, "Okay," again. I rounded the car and saw the husband leaned over the steering wheel inside. Beth stood a few feet away, her eyes closed and calm. "Evie, come over here and hold my hand. I'm going to try to reach through and touch him."

Evie placed her hand in mine and then together, we pressed against the car window. As the window moved under our hands, something hit me from behind, knocking my breath out of me and my hand from Evie's.

I whirled around and felt the onslaught as Beth came at me, her eyes wild and her hair flying around her face.

"Stop!" I yelled.

Evie backed away. "What's happening?"

Andy and Tristan were next to me, attempting to shield me from the unseen danger.

Beth grabbed hold of me, pulling me toward the place she stood before. I could see a black mist wrapped around her ankles, a thick, ominous rope of pain. She yanked again, pulling me from Andy and Tristan's grasp and then I was skidding across the ground, headed for a circle made of the broken pieces of car that had come off in the wreck. The black mist strung from Beth to the center of the circle. I planted my feet on the ground and dug in my heels and Beth hesitated. She turned baleful eyes in my direction and in the moonlight, I could see that her pupils had taken over her entire eyes - an inky blackness lay beyond her lashes.

Andy's hands were on my shoulders then and he leaned back, pulling at me as Beth played tug of war with my legs. He was no match for her strength and I began moving again, slowly edging toward the circle.

"Tristan! Grab her arm!" Andy's voice was loud in my ear. "Patton! Get over here!"

I turned to see Evie standing several feet behind, rooted to the spot. Her eyes were wide and her mouth was open. I followed her gaze as Tristan placed his hands on my other arm, holding me as Beth tugged me closer.

Sam stood in the clearing near the circle. His head was lowered and his eyes never left Beth as he chanted something under his breath.

"Sam!" I screamed. "Sam! Help me!"

His focus faltered for the smallest of seconds and then his shoulders rose as he took a deep breath and began chanting again.

Evie passed into my line of vision, walking slowly toward the vision of Sam.

"Evie! No!"

Beth pulled again, her mouth spreading into a slow smile as the toes of my shoes came within inches of the circle on the ground. Andy and Tristan yanked me back and I felt like I was going to split in half.

"You have to get Evie away," I said.

"No way we're leaving you," Andy panted.

"Evie!" I shouted again.

She half-turned and looked at me. "It's Sam?"

"It's not him," I cried. "It's him but it's not. Something's wrong." I turned to Beth. "Beth, if you are still in there, please stop this. Brandon wouldn't want you to do this."

At the mention of her husband, her grip faltered and her eyes shifted back to normal. "Brandon?"

"Yes, Beth, Brandon wouldn't want you to do this. We're trying to help."

She narrowed her eyes. "You tried to help before. He told me that I could make all the pain and sadness stop, and that's exactly what I'm doing."

"He's lying, Beth. I don't know what he told you, but doing this isn't going to help."

She paused, looking past me at her husband's form trapped in the car. A guttural noise echoed up from her core, spreading out into the quiet night.

"Beth, please," I whispered.

She glared at me and then let go, turning as she did so and jettisoning into the circle. The black smoke followed her, disappearing into the hard ground, sending the circle's shards of glass and metal out in an explosion. Sam roared and lunged toward me. Evie stood in the space between and placed her hands up in front of her. The action drove Sam back to the edge of the woods. He paced back and forth, like a caged animal, attempting to push past Evie's influence.

She turned her head a bit and spoke over her shoulder. "Get St. Louis out of here," she said, her voice calm and steady.

"No, Evie!"

"Get her out of here now!"

Andy and Tristan pulled me to my feet and backpedaled up the embankment, holding onto me. My eyes never left Evie as she stood stoic in the space below.

Suddenly, she whirled around and started running toward us. "Get in the cars! Now!"

Sam threw himself at her retreating form and black smoke emanated from him. It swiped at Evie's back as she ran. She cried out in pain and shot forward, running for all she was worth.

A sonic boom and then Sam was gone, the ground where he was standing charred and smoking.

Andy ran across the road with me in tow, and practically shoved me into the truck. He leapt in and turned the engine over, flooding my car in the headlights. We waited for Evie and Tristan to get into my car and pull out onto the road. As soon as they did, Andy hit the gas, his truck fishtailing as he punched it down the highway after them.

I turned around in the seat and stared at the road disappearing behind us. No one was following, but I found myself turning to check long after I had buckled in and we were far up the highway.

My breath came in bursts and I shivered. My legs hurt where Beth held onto them. Panicked, I asked Andy to turn on the cab light. He obliged and I stared down at my legs, terrified that I would see the black smoke wound around them. I tilted my head and squinted, feeling along my shins. Nothing. I almost cried with relief.

"It's okay. You can turn the light off now," I said, as Andy followed Tristan and Evie onto the road that ran in front of our house.

He turned off the light and glanced over at me. "What the heck happened out there? Was Sam really there?"

"I don't think that thing was Sam," I whispered.

CHAPTER 15

Tears streamed down Evie's face as Tristan helped her out of my car. Andy parked next to them in the driveway and killed the engine. I hopped out and ran around to unlock the back door. Andy and Tristan helped Evie up the steps and into the kitchen. I held the door open wide for them and then closed and locked it behind them, dropping my backpack by the fridge. Skirting around the form of my grandma, I grabbed a clean towel from the drawer and ran it under cold water in the sink. Andy and Tristan lowered Evie into a chair and I squeezed out the extra water and brought it over to her.

"Evie? Can I see the scratch?"

She looked up at me, her eyes red-rimmed.

I took the towel and gently wiped the tears from her cheeks. "Come on, let me see."

She pulled up the hem of her shirt. I moved around to look at her back and my hand flew up to my mouth. There, among the old scratches were four fresh red ones, rising in angry welts and weeping droplets of blood along their length.

"Oh, Evie," Tristan breathed.

I blinked to clear my head and then placed the towel on the area that looked the worst at the top near her neck.

"Hey, look what the cat dragged in. He came home to surprise you…" My dad stopped in the doorway, his eyes quickly taking in the situation. Grant stood at his side, the smile fading on his face.

It took me a second for Grant's presence to register. *What is he doing here?* I cleared my throat and looked at my dad.

"What happened?" Dad pushed his glasses up on his nose and walked over. Andy and Tristan moved back, giving him room.

I handed him the towel. It was stained pink with Evie's blood. "We were trying to help a ghost and Sam showed up and…" I stopped, taking a deep breath as Grant took my shaking hand.

Dad turned to look at me, his eyes blazing. "Who is this Sam?"

The aroma of biscuits baking in the oven filled my senses. I sat down heavily in the chair next to Evie. "Sam is a ghost that helped to save Evie when she was in a coma. He died a long time ago in the courthouse and he helped her get back into her body." I left out the part where he was tricked into allowing the dark spirit to take Evie as a trap for me.

Dad turned his attention back to Evie. "Do you mind if I take a look at your back, Genevieve?"

She shook her head and placed it in the crook of her arms lying on the tabletop.

"Marissa, go upstairs and get the first aid kit out of my bathroom. Grant, Andy, and Tristan, I'm sure Genevieve would appreciate some privacy."

"Um, yeah." Andy grabbed Tristan by the arm and jerked his head toward the living room. Grant followed them and I ran up the stairs, yanking open the closet door in Dad's bathroom and searching the shelves for the kit. I found it and headed back downstairs.

When I got back into the kitchen, Evie's sobs had ebbed and Dad was gently washing the blood away from the wounds. He spoke to her softly and didn't look up as I handed him the first aid kit. I wrapped my arms around myself and backed away, standing near the counter. I could hear the rumble of the boys talking in the living room and shook my head.

"Dad, I'm sorry. I didn't realize that she'd get hurt."

"Not now, Marissa."

I blinked back tears and pressed my lips together.

"Come help me."

I walked over and spread the antiseptic cream along the scratches. We unrolled some gauze and placed it gently on her back, holding it in place with white medical tape. I rolled her shirt down and gulped when I saw the rips in the T shirt.

"Come upstairs with me and we'll get you a new shirt, okay?"

She nodded numbly and stood up, allowing me to lead her upstairs. I deposited her on my bed, ran into her room, and grabbed a new T shirt from her dresser drawer. In my room again, I helped her out of her ripped shirt and into the new one. I sat down on the bed next to her and smoothed her hair away from her face.

"Evie, are you okay?"

She turned to look at me. "I'm okay." Her voice was quiet but strong.

I sat looking down at my feet hanging off the edge of the bed for a long time. Finally, Evie's voice broke the silence.

She closed her eyes. "He's still in there, St. Louis. I *know* he is."

"That's *not* Sam anymore. Did you see him?"

She shook her head. "I'm only able to see his outline. He's got an awful greenish grey color around him." She opened her eyes and looked over at me. "Something's making him act like this. Sam would never hurt me."

"But, he *has*."

Her bottom lip trembled.

"Evie, how many times have you tried to talk to him?"

She blinked and shook her head.

A quiet knock sounded on my door. Andy leaned his head in. "Can we join the party?"

Evie nodded.

"Yeah, come on in," I said. Andy and Tristan filed in, followed by Grant and my dad.

"We ordered pizza," Andy said, "and it should be here soon."

Dad handed Evie an open can of soda and then sat down on my office chair. Andy and Tristan sat on the futon and Grant leaned against the doorjamb. No one spoke for a long time.

Dad cleared his throat. "You know I have to know what's going on now, right? The promise was that no one else would get hurt and you didn't keep up your end of the deal." His eyes bore into me.

I winced at his words and nodded. "Sam Johnson died during the construction of the courthouse in 1904.

He is still hanging around and we contacted him with a spirit board that Evie found at an antique store. He and Evie got to be really good friends and when she was in a coma, she got to know him even better and," I turned to look at her, "I think she kind of fell for him."

Dad moved his head up and down slowly, opening a butterscotch candy and popping it into his mouth. "Did Sam hurt you while you were a ghost?"

"No, sir," Evie said. "He was gentle and kind and funny."

"Then what happened?"

"We think he got taken by a bad spirit."

Dad sat back and looked up at the ceiling. "A bad spirit."

"Under the courthouse, there's a bad spirit that lives in the basement," Andy offered.

"And why do you think it lives there?"

"Because Marissa saw it."

I looked at Andy, my eyes wide.

"Sorry," he mumbled.

"The basement was filled in during the nineties," Dad said. "How did you get down there?"

"Um, there's a cave system that runs under the courthouse."

Dad swung his eyes down and stared at me. "You went into the *caves?*" He swept a hand back through his hair. "Do you know how dangerous that is? People get lost down there and never come out."

"Sam led us. He knows the caves."

Dad leaned forward and rested his elbows on his knees. He tented his hands and placed his chin on them. "You do know I'd give my right arm for you guys to have normal teenage problems, right? Anyone got relationship problems? Someone you know on drugs? A teacher being unfair about grades?" He shook his head. "Those I would know how to handle. This, *this* stuff is something completely outside of my wheelhouse."

"And you think it's in mine?" I snapped. "I never asked for any of this! I never asked to see ghosts or have my friend get hurt or stand in a cave and face the darkest things I've ever imagined!"

Everyone in the room was quiet, and I felt their eyes watching me.

Dad held up his hand. "That's fair. No, you didn't ask for any of this, and I want you to stop. I don't want you going on ghost hunts anymore. It stops tonight."

Andy leaned forward. "Mr. Anderson, but we have…"

Dad stood up. "No, you don't have anything. I am not your parent, but I am Marissa's and I'm as close to a parent as Genevieve has, and I am putting my foot down. This has gotten way out of hand and it stops. *Tonight."* With that, Dad turned on his heel and headed out of the room. Grant moved out of his way as he passed. His footsteps pounded down the steps.

"Whoa," Andy said, "that was intense."

"He's scared," Evie said from her spot next to me on the bed.

I stood up. "I'm going to go talk to him."

Grant stopped me at the door. "Do you want me to go down there with you?"

I shook my head, my eyes filling with tears. "I'm so sorry about all of this. Maybe you should leave?"

He smiled and brought my hand to his lips. "Nah, I've cleared my schedule for this tonight. I'll be right here if you need me."

"St. Louis?"

I turned to look at Evie.

She scooted up to the edge of the bed. "His colors…he's hiding something, too."

I went down the stairs. Dad was in his office sitting behind his desk, his chair turned backwards, staring out the window at the darkness. The sun set almost an hour before. We planned to go out to Kristen's tonight and I had to get Dad to relent before he would allow me out of the house again. I walked in and sat down in one of his leather wingback chairs, drawing my knees up under me.

"Did you find that Dad speech on the Internet?"

He chuckled and swung his chair around. "I'm not mad at you, you know."

"I know. Evie says you're scared."

Dad stared at me for a moment. Then he took a deep breath. "I suppose I am scared. I'm scared that something will happen to you."

I squinted. "It feels like more than that."

Just then, the doorbell rang.

Dad pushed his chair back and stood up. "I don't want to talk about this anymore tonight, Peanut. Leave it alone, okay?"

I stood up and followed him to the front door. He pulled his wallet out of his back pocket and flipped on the porch light. He opened the door and froze.

Melanie stood out on the front porch, her hat askew on her head and a bright pink pocketbook roughly the size of Oregon clutched to her chest.

"Johnny?" she said, her eyes flashing in the light. "Johnny, I'm ready to listen now."

CHAPTER 16

The five of us sat on the couches in the living room in silence, munching on the pizza that was delivered a few minutes after Melanie showed up. She and Dad had retreated into the kitchen and I heard him put on a fresh pot of coffee.

I looked over at Evie and raised my eyebrows. She shrugged.

Grant sat next to me on the couch, his hand draped lightly on my leg. The warmth that radiated from his palm was comforting and I leaned into his side a bit more.

"What do you think they're talking about?" Tristan asked.

I shook my head. "I have no idea. She said that she was ready to listen to him now. I think it has something to do with how her son died."

Andy glanced at his watch. "What time did you tell Kristen we'd be there?"

"I didn't give her a time." I pulled my phone out. "She never texted back. I mean, I guess it's okay if we go out there, right?"

"We can drive by and make sure she's alone. If her husband's car is there, we'll have to try again," Andy said.

"We should probably go pretty soon," Evie said.

Andy smiled. "You're not going anywhere tonight, Patton."

Evie bristled. "I'm fine."

"Are you going to tell them?" I asked.

She stared at me, and then sighed. "I've tried to talk to Sam. Before."

"I saw the old scratches," Tristan said. "Did he do that to you, too?"

Evie looked down at her hands folded in her lap. "It's not his fault."

"It's not okay for him to hurt you," Andy said. He put his arm around her shoulders and hugged her to him gently. "You have to stop this."

"Where do you think you see him?" I asked.

"The cave. I'm just trying to help him like he helped me."

"It's too dangerous, Evie. It's not him anymore."

"He's being controlled by the darkness," she mumbled. "It's making him do these things." She looked up and around the room. "It can make you do things."

"What things? What can it make you do?" I asked. I leaned up and looked across the coffee table at her. "Do you remember what it was like when you were down there?"

Evie nodded, a lone tear escaping and rolling down her cheek.

"Can you talk about it?" I whispered.

Her tear-filled eyes were wide with fright and sadness. She shook her head in a minute motion. "It hurts too much."

"What are the circles?" Andy asked.

Evie looked at him gratefully.

Tristan pulled out his phone. "I was thinking about this earlier." He scrolled through the screens. "There's a theory out there that people can build portals to interact with the dead."

I furrowed my brow. "I've heard that some places can be portals, but those are naturally occurring."

"Some are naturally occurring, and some people have used mirrors to tap into portals. I found this video and it shows how a person *built* a portal to the other side. Here." He pulled up the video and turned his phone so that we could all see it.

Words flashed across a black background. *This is found footage. Leslie Davis, nineteen-year-old college student is considered missing at this time. Please contact local authorities at the number listed below if you have knowledge of her whereabouts.* The screen faded to black and then more words appeared. *The following events occurred on December 14, 2013. View at your own risk.* On the screen, a young woman with long dark hair stood in the woods. She was dressed in a flowing brown dress and had several beaded necklaces hanging from her neck.

"Hi, y'all, Leslie here and today I'm going to show you how to open a portal to the other side. Now, I've gathered some stones and laid them out here on the ground." She reached out and picked up the camera. It swung around. There was a lot of movement, and then the lens focused on the cleared place on the ground. Stones were laid in a perfect circle. "You can do this with any material, but something from the earth usually works best." Steam filled the screen as she spoke. Then, the camera angle swung around again as she placed it down and stepped back, leaning in front of the camera to make sure she was in the shot. "This spell works best during the winter. I've tried it in the summer and I usually have pretty poor results. So, I've cleared the area, put the stones in a circle, and now I'm ready to invoke the portal." She stared up at the bare treetops, the steam of her breath escaping in a cloud as she breathed out.

A rustling wound its way through the trees and she looked over her shoulder. She stood still, the noise finally stopping. She turned to face the camera again. "A friendly little woodland creature must be wondering what I'm doing," she smiled. "Go ahead and kneel down by the northernmost part of your circle and get comfortable." She knelt with her back to the woods and adjusted her skirt, placing it in a wide arc around her on the ground. She took a deep breath and closed her eyes. "Spirits of the other world, please allow me entrance into your realm. Allow me entrance as a visitor in pure love and pure light." The camera shook and then went black.

"What happened?" I whispered.

"Just watch," Tristan said.

A moment later, the camera turned on and Leslie sat back on her knees again. The wind picked up and the tree branches swung in the frame behind her. The rustling noise began again and she looked behind her, her long hair spilling over her shoulder. When the wind died down, she turned back to the camera. "That was weird." Her smile this time was tight with anxiety. She closed her eyes and began the invocation again. As she did, a shadow moved into the frame, dancing along the edge of the woods, not taking shape, but watching, and waiting.

Leslie continued her chant and a whisper of a mist grew in the middle of the circle. It made itself into a rope and then snaked out to the forest, hovering around the trees. A moment later, the camera shut itself off again.

None of us breathed in the living room as we watched the black screen for almost thirty seconds. Then, the camera flashed on, blacked out, and then flashed on again. It was on its side and the stones were scattered. Leslie was gone.

"It goes on like that for another thirty minutes, but nothing else happens. Then, the camera shows a low battery and eventually shuts off."

"What happened to her?" I asked, rubbing the goosebumps from my arms.

"She's still reported as a missing person in Indiana."

"Well, that doesn't necessarily mean the portal worked," Andy said. "Maybe a bear ate her."

"According to predator maps, it was more likely a bobcat or coyote pack in that area of the country."

The group looked at me and I shrugged. "I'm afraid of getting eaten by something," I said.

"The question of whether or not she got the portal to work aside, if Marissa has seen ghosts building portals, I want to know why." Tristan swiped at his phone and put it back in his pocket.

"And I want to know if there are more," I said.

Just then, Melanie came into the room, the color high on her cheeks. She stopped in front of the door.

I stood up and walked over to her. "Is everything okay?"

She shook her head and smashed her hat down on her head. I helped her into her coat.

"He won't listen to me. Maybe you'll get through to him," she said. She pulled the photo of my dad and her son from her bag and handed it to me. "Good luck, dear."

I opened the door for her and watched as she climbed into her car. I closed the door as she drove away. Then I turned around.

Dad stood in the doorway. "I'll be in my office," he said. His voice sounded defeated, sad. It reminded me of the way he sounded when my mom was sick and Evie had been in the coma.

I followed him, holding the frame to my side.

"We'll clean up," Evie offered.

"Thanks," I said over my shoulder.

Dad sat leaned over his desk, his head in his hands.

I let myself in and closed the windowed doors behind me. "Are you okay?"

Dad looked up at me and shook his head. "I thought I left all of this behind."

"What did Melanie say to you?" I perched on the edge of the chair cushion.

He sighed. "She wanted to talk about the day that Thomas died."

I ducked my head to catch his gaze. "What happened that day? Why won't you talk about it?"

His eyes filled with tears and he rubbed a hand across the stubble on his chin. "I don't know if I *can* talk about it."

I licked my lips and sat up even more. "Dad, we have to go to Kristen's house tonight. She said that the doll is back and that her little girl is scared. We have to help her."

"Nope, no, you don't. You don't have to help them, *any* of them."

"Yes, I do! They're crying out for help and I think I'm the only one that can help them. I *have* to."

He slammed his hand down on the desk and I jumped. The noises coming from the living room paused for a moment and then continued.

Dad put his head in his hands again. "I'm sorry, but this time you're wrong, Marissa. You can't help them."

"But, I'm the only one who can see them!"

"You can turn it off." He looked up at me, his eyes blazing. "I did."

I stared across the desk at my dad, the enormity of what he was saying hitting me like a truck. I squinted. "You can see them, too?"

He stood up, pacing behind his desk. "Not anymore. I shut that part off a long time ago and I suggest you do the same."

I placed the photo on the desk and turned it his way. "You shut that part off, but I won't." I stood up and faced my dad. "I can't do that. Not now. There are too many people that need my help. We are going to Kristen's house and we are going to help this little girl. Now, I will text you when we get there and I will text you every single half hour if you want me to, but we are going and there's nothing you can do to stop me."

I waited and watched to see how my act of complete defiance would be received. This was unchartered territory in our relationship and I held my breath, waiting for him to say something.

He sat down hard in his chair, staring at the picture, his eyes seeming deeper in his eye sockets. He ran a hand through his hair. "I tried to help him."

CHAPTER 17

"I'm sorry, Dad. Do you want to talk about it?"

He stared at the picture for a minute more and then he nodded his head. "I'm going to get a cup of coffee and then I'll tell you what happened." He stood up and came around the desk. He stood in front of me and then gathered me in a hug. "I love you so much, Peanut."

"I love you, too," I said into his flannel shirt.

Dad went into the kitchen where my friends were putting things from dinner away. He poured a cup of coffee. "I suppose Marissa will tell you everything I'm about to tell you, so I'll cut out the middle man. Meet me in the living room."

Evie furrowed her brow and looked at me. I jerked my head toward the living room and they all filed in, finding a spot on the couches. Dad pulled a chair in from the dining room and sat down on it. The wood creaked as he leaned back and put a foot up on his opposite knee.

"I used to be able to see ghosts, too," he started, "as Marissa can. When I was little, I used to see spirits when we went to church and in places around town. I thought everyone could do it. It wasn't until my mother told me that the other kids would think I was strange if I talked about it. So, I hid it. I didn't tell anyone. I could still see ghosts but I didn't acknowledge them. It got easier to ignore them after a while. It was almost as if the more I ignored them, the less I had the ability to see them." He took a sip of coffee. "Melanie's son, Thomas, and I practically grew up together. We were best friends and did everything together. We were in all the same classes at school and hung out almost every weekend."

"Did he know you could see ghosts?" I asked, thinking of Piper, my best friend from back home. I never told her what I could do. In fact, I didn't tell anyone until I met Evie.

Dad shook his head. "No. By the time I was in high school, the ability was practically gone."

"How about now?" I asked, glancing at the kitchen where the smell of bacon was thick in the air.

"Not at all, and I don't want it."

"What happened to Thomas?" I asked.

"When we graduated, we went out and bought that car. It was a classic 1956 Pontiac Chieftain. We pooled every last cent we had and bought it from Old Joe McClellan at the junkyard. We got it home and started restoring it in Thomas' driveway. It took us the rest of the summer, but we finally got it up and running." He smiled, a wistful quality covering his features. Then, they hardened and he cleared his throat. "We took the car out for a ride. Thomas was driving and we were out on Big Plank Road. It was gravel back then and he was driving too fast. We hit a curve and he lost control. It all happened so fast and then the car rolled down the embankment and landed in the lake." Dad stopped and stared off into space. He blinked and looked around at us. "We hit the water and the windshield cracked. Water poured in and filled up the car in a matter of seconds. I was having trouble getting the lift latch up on my seatbelt and Thomas pulled his pocketknife out and cut it for me. I kicked out the side window and waited until he was unbuckled. Then, I went through the window and swam up to the surface."

He swallowed, his Adam's apple moving up and down several times. When he spoke again, his voice was filled with emotion. "Thomas didn't come up. I took a breath and swam back down, but the car had flipped over and was going down fast. It was kicking up so much mud that the water was almost black. I swam down three more times but I couldn't get down far enough. That part of the lake was nearly fifty feet deep. When the police came, they pulled me out and sent in divers. They never found his body." Dad stopped talking, took off his glasses, and rubbed his hand over his eyes, squeezing his fingers on the bridge of his nose.

"That's awful," I said.

He looked over at me. "I used to visit him. He would be sitting there on the bank, staring out over the water. For a long time, I didn't try to talk to him. I sat there next to my best friend and stared out over the lake. He said one thing over and over again, 'Tell my mom that I love her.'" He sighed. "I went to Melanie about a week after the accident and tried to talk to her, tell her that he was okay and that he loved her. She shut the door in my face. The last thing she said to me was, 'I didn't even have a body to bury.'"

Dad shifted in his seat. "So, I went back to the lake. I thought if I was able to get his body out of the car, I could help her grieve." He shook his head. "It was stupid, but I wasn't thinking clearly. I got out there, took off my shoes and got ready to dive into the water, and I tried repeatedly. I couldn't find the car, him, or anything. So, I sat down on the bank next to him and I cried. I told him that I missed him and then I yelled at him. I was so darn mad that he had saved me and not gotten out himself. That wasn't the way things were supposed to go. We were supposed to get jobs together and get married to the prettiest girls in town and watch our kids play together. One of us wasn't supposed to be dead. That wasn't the deal. I-I got so mad at him that he couldn't hear me that I shoved him. Then for a moment, he could see me. He looked up at me like he'd been in a trance and I'd shaken him out of it."

Dad's chin quivered and I thought I was going to lose it. Grant reached over and took my hand.

"He changed, then, didn't he?" I said, my eyes burning with tears.

Dad regarded me for a moment. "Yeah, all of a sudden, he turned blue and his eyes bugged out from their sockets. His skin turned white and papery and sloughed off in places. He opened his mouth and a gurgling sound came out." Dad lifted the mug to his lips with a shaking hand. "I left. I got in my car and drove away and I've never been back. I shut that part of myself off that day and I never looked back. I came home, got in a huge fight with my dad, and told him I was leaving for college. I packed up my bags that very day and left town." He leaned forward. "So, when I tell you that things are better left alone, I know what I'm talking about."

I took a deep breath. "Something like that happened to me." I told him about Red and how I thought I'd completely messed things up. "But, Melanie was able to tell him what he needed and he was able to go back to before, when he was happy. You can still do that for Thomas. You can erase the bad stuff and he'll be back to staring out over the lake."

Dad stared at me, a strange expression on his face. "You know, for someone who says she's afraid of everything, you're so much braver than me."

"It's okay. We can get Melanie and take her out there. She can talk to him through me and he can tell her the message he wanted to tell her. It'll fix everything. I promise."

Dad snorted. "You think it will be that easy, huh?"

I looked at Andy and Tristan warily. *As long as Sam doesn't show up.* "I do. Call Melanie and tell her that you need to talk. We can go tomorrow."

"I will. You guys had better hurry and get out to Kristen's. It's getting pretty late." He stood up and returned the chair to the dining room table. "Text me every half hour," he said over his shoulder.

CHAPTER 18

I followed the red taillights of Andy's truck as they floated through the dust cloud in front of me on the labyrinth of back country roads toward Kristen's house. Andy, Tristan, and Evie were in the truck and Grant and I took my car. I glanced over at him in my passenger seat.

"Why didn't you tell me that you were coming home this weekend?" I asked, turning down the radio.

He chuckled. "I wanted to surprise you. I missed you." He reached over and laid his hand on mine as it rested on the gear shift. He gave my hand a small squeeze.

"Bet you wish you'd stayed at school after all this tonight."

"Are you kidding? This is the most excitement I've had all week! Seriously, I've been going to classes and studying. I needed the break."

"I'm glad you came." I glanced over at him again. "Really, it means a lot that you're doing this with me."

"Wouldn't miss it. So, tell me what's going to happen when we get there."

"Well, we'll go in and talk to Kristen and see what's been going on lately. We thought burying Amalie with her family would stop all of the activity in the house, but Kristen texted that the doll was back even though I left it on Amalie's grave."

Grant was quiet for a moment. "And, you're not creeped out by any of that?"

I smiled and turned onto another gravel road. "I'm creeped out, but I want to find out why the doll is back. Does that mean that Amalie is still in the house, and if she is, why?"

"Can you talk to her?"

I squinted. "Kind of. She speaks in German."

"Wow."

"Well, yeah. I mean, she's an old ghost."

"What should I watch out for?"

"What do you mean?"

He cleared his throat. "I want to know what to watch for so I can help you if I need to. Like, will you pass out or fall down?"

"I'll get tired. Interacting with spirits taps my energy, but it shouldn't be too bad. I've learned when I'm pushing myself too far."

Grant was quiet for a while.

"What are you thinking?" I asked.

"That you're about the coolest person I've ever met."

I snorted. "Right. Cool. That's a word everyone uses to describe me. We're here." I followed Andy's truck into the driveway and pulled up beside him next to the shed. I texted my dad to let him know that we'd gotten to Kristen's. We all piled out of the vehicles and stood in the starless night. I wrapped my coat around me and turned my collar up against the bitter wind.

"Where's Kristen's car?" Andy asked.

I looked up at the house. There were no lights on and it stood dark in the quiet night.

"Something's wrong. I don't think they're home," I said.

Andy opened the toolbox on his truck and pulled out his bag. He reached inside and started passing out flashlights. I tested mine and then swung the beam up to one of the front windows. The light reflected off the dark glass.

"What do you see?" I asked Evie.

She cocked her head to the side and stared at the house. "Nothing, I don't see anything at all." She turned to me. "That's weird."

"Yeah." I tried to keep the tremor out of my voice, but it shook anyway. "Come on." I led the way up to the porch and reached out to ring the doorbell. It didn't work. We stood still, listening for any movement beyond. Nothing.

"Try the door," Andy suggested.

I reached out with a gloved hand and turned the knob. The latch clicked and the door swung out of my hand, carried on the wind blowing from our backs. It hit the wall on the other side and bounced back, nearly closing again. The house was dark beyond and I forced myself to reach inside and feel along the wall for a light switch. I couldn't find one and yanked off my glove with my other hand before reaching in again. This time, my fingers found the switch and I held my breath and pushed it up. Nothing. I tried once more. No light.

"Perfect," I whispered.

"Flashlights on," Andy said and clicked his, holding it under his chin. "Mwahahaha!"

"Knock it off," Tristan said.

I leaned in and called out, my voice carrying on the wind. "Kristen? Hannah? Um, Amalie?" When there was no response, I pushed the door open wide and stepped into the foyer. I swung the beam of my flashlight around the quiet living room.

"Maybe they went out for dinner?" Evie said from right behind me.

"It feels...more empty..." I said.

The group stepped in behind me, and with the extra light from their flashlights, I was able to get a good look at the living room. The Christmas tree stood in the corner near the fireplace but the couch and chair were missing. We walked through to the kitchen and found the kitchen table and chairs gone, and all of the cabinet doors were open. Some were filled with plates and glasses, and some stood empty.

"Same thing in the pantry," Andy said. "Also, you guys should come see this."

We all crowded into the pantry and looked at the basement door. On it was the padlock that had been there when we visited last, but now, there were three more locks added, and a board lying on the floor from the door to the opposite wall, effectively barring the door from opening.

"They didn't want that door opened," Evie stated.

"This is really strange. I'm going to text Kristen." I pulled out my phone. *We're at your house. Is everything okay?*

"Do you think they were robbed?" Andy asked. He opened the refrigerator and immediately shut it again. "*I* wouldn't even eat any of that."

"No, it feels like they've been gone for longer." I counted for a minute. "It's been a little over a week since we were out here and she texted me that night with the picture of the doll. I texted her this week, but haven't heard back from her."

There was a thumping sound upstairs and Evie squeaked and stood closer to Andy. I moved my flashlight to the stairs in the living room.

Grant touched my arm. "Do you want me to go first?"

I smiled. "We can go together."

"I think I might throw up," Evie said.

"You want to go first?" I asked.

Her eyes widened and she shook her head. "Not until we find out where that creepy doll is."

I walked into the living room and pointed my light up the stairs, as Grant and I climbed the first three steps side by side. Andy, Evie, and Tristan followed close behind. As we crested the landing, there was another thump and then the sound of a door closing. I placed a foot in the upstairs hallway.

Grant grabbed my elbow and pulled me back. "I don't like this," he said. "If they were robbed, the guy could still be in the house," he whispered.

Good point. "Fine," I whispered, and then gestured to the group to go back downstairs.

We got to the living room and moved quietly out to the front porch.

"Should we call the sheriff?" Tristan asked. His phone was already out of his pocket.

I shook my head and looked back at the house. "I don't think it's anything living."

"Oh, please sign me up to go back in," Evie groused.

"Someone's coming," Andy tilted his head toward the gravel road in front of the house.

Headlights crested the hill and drove past. I held my breath as the vehicle passed and then stopped. It sat still on the road for a moment and then the sound of a gear shift and the truck's reverse lights lit up the road in front of the house.

"Crap," Grant said.

"It's okay. We're not doing anything wrong."

"Only breaking and entering. That looks great on a college application," Tristan said under his breath.

The pickup truck backed up past the driveway and then pulled in, stopping right next to my car. The engine turned off and a man stepped out.

"What are you kids doing out here?"

"Mr. Brown?" Tristan moved out of our group and walked down the porch steps. He looked back over his shoulder. "It's my grandpa's friend."

"Hey, there, Tristan. What's got you out here tonight?" The old man stood leaning on the open door of his truck.

I could make out the figure of a woman sitting in the passenger side. She waved and I lifted my hand in a wave back to her.

"You can see her, right?" I said out of the corner of my mouth to Evie.

"Yep. Living."

Tristan walked over and shook Mr. Brown's hand. "We were on our way home from getting a burger in Eagleton and we were driving past the house and thought we saw someone run inside. There weren't any cars in the driveway and we thought maybe we should call the sheriff to make sure the family that lives here is safe."

Mr. Brown peered up at the house, and pushed his hat back on his head. "Well, that's strange. The family that lived here, the Lindemanns, picked up and moved out in a hurry on, hmmm, when was that, Susan?" He leaned into the truck.

"I heard that from Jenny down at the salon on, I think it was Monday."

"Monday. That sounds right."

"Where did they go?" Andy asked, walking up to stand next to Tristan. We joined him.

"No idea. They lit out of here with what they could pack into her car and his truck. The Young family," Mr. Brown jerked his thumb over his shoulder at the house a bit down the road, "said that they heard that little girl crying all the way to their house. She was screaming her head off about a doll that she didn't want to leave behind. Mrs. Young drove her golf cart up here to see if she could help, and Mr. Lindemann handed her the keys and told her that they were leaving. She said they looked scared to death."

Andy tossed a meaningful look over at us.

Tristan pulled out his phone. "Well, we're getting ready to call the sheriff."

Mr. Brown swept his hand down in a stiff motion. "Nah, don't bother Rusty tonight. He's over helping the state police run a checkpoint on Highway 36. I'll go in with you." He reached into the truck and pulled a shotgun down from the gun rack above the seat. He snapped it open and looked down the barrel. He passed the truck keys to his wife. "Why don't you drive over to the Youngs' house and get the keys? Come on, then," he said to us as he walked over to the porch.

"The electricity is off inside," Tristan mentioned.

"Huh." Mr. Brown stopped. "I doubt they took the time to turn off the electricity yet. We'll check the breaker."

We followed Mr. Brown into the house, probably way too close. Our huddle stayed tight behind him as he stepped into the house and looked around the living room.

"Where's the breaker?" Evie asked.

"Most likely down in the basement," he said.

Tristan led him to the kitchen. "The basement door's in here, but I'm not sure we'll be able to get down there."

Mr. Brown went into the pantry and reached back to Tristan for his flashlight. "Probably right down these steps," he said, disappearing into the basement.

Andy swung his flashlight beam to the doorjamb. The padlocks were all ripped from the door, their bright brass plates hanging askew from the splintered wood.

"Look at this," Evie said. She shined her flashlight at the floor. The board had been broken in half, the jagged edges of wood leaving splinters on the floor.

"Here it is," Mr. Brown's voice wound up the stairs. There was a metallic clang and then the sound of the breaker being clicked.

All of a sudden, the entire house came to life. The lights sprung up around us and every small appliance in the kitchen began whirring. Grant, Evie, and I went around unplugging all of them, dampening the noise a bit. Other things were running in the house and we stood in the kitchen looking around us. Another thump from upstairs.

"Well, if there is anyone in the house, we just scared the crap out of him," Andy said.

Mr. Brown's boots scuffed up the stairs. He stood at the top and pulled the chain to turn off the light in the pantry.

"Any other rooms down here?" he asked.

I shook my head. "A bathroom by the stairs and a couple of closets."

He walked past the back door and yanked on the knob a few times. "Locked."

He nodded his head toward the living room and we all followed him into the space. Evie and I pulled open doors and checked the interiors before turning off the lights. Music lilted in the quiet house, carrying down the stairs to us.

"I'm going to head upstairs," Mr. Brown said. "You kids can stay down here if you want."

"I'll come with you," Tristan said. He looked at me.

"Me, too," I said.

"I'll stay here with this chicken," Andy said, leaning his head toward Evie. He smiled at Grant. "You can go with your chicken."

I tossed a glare at Andy and then climbed the stairs. The music was louder at the top and sounded like it was coming from Hannah's parents' room. Tristan stopped at the first room, Hannah's, and Mr. Brown went in. He looked around, and then he exited, moving down the hallway toward Kristen and Dalton's room. The room felt like the aftermath of a tornado. Toys lay strewn on the floor and all of the drawers in the dresser were open, clothing spilling out from their mostly empty interiors. The bed was not made and it looked like Hannah had been sleeping when her parents pulled her out of the bed. I walked around, looking for any sign of the doll. Tristan got down and looked under the bed, shaking his head as he stood up again.

He hesitated at the door. "Closet?" he asked.

"Um, yeah."

Grant stood between us. "What does he mean?" he asked.

"I found Amalie hiding in her closet last time we were here."

"I'll go with you." Grant said to me as Tristan followed Mr. Brown down the hall.

I smiled. "You can't fit. Besides, I'm not scared. She won't hurt me. She's just scared."

Grant shook his head. "This is going to get easier to understand, won't it?"

I grabbed his hand and squeezed. "Not likely."

He chuckled.

As I opened the closet door, I heard the music stop further up the hallway. The entire house took on an eerie stillness. The light was on in her closet and several empty purple plastic hangers swung from the rack. A few lone shoes lay on the floor, their matches probably hundreds of miles away by now. The entire house had the feel of a hasty getaway and it was deeply unsettling. *What happened here? What made them leave? Why were they so scared?*

I pushed my way into the closet and got down on my hands and knees. I made the familiar journey to the end of the closet and held my breath as I pointed my flashlight into the space. There was a moment of heart-stopping fear as I closed my eyes and then opened them, moving my body so I could peer around the corner.

Amalie's secret room looked completely untouched. The lamp sat at the far end, spilling a warm yellow light into the space. Her books lay abandoned on the floor, and the blanket and pillow were stacked neatly at the edge of the space. There was no feeling, no whisper of life or spirit here. *The house was dead.* That's why it felt so wrong. *Why wasn't I seeing her family?* My phone buzzed from my pocket and the sound jolted me. I sat up quickly, smacking the back of my head on the small doorframe.

"You okay?" Grant asked from the door of the closet behind me.

"Yeah, help me out." I held my hand out to him and he pulled, helping me stand up when I got to her room. I got my phone out and stared down at the screen. It was a video from Kristen with two sentences. *Dalton believes me now. Get out of the house.*

I pulled up the video and watched as it showed the upstairs hallway. It was dark and I could hear scared breathing on the screen. I bumped up the sound a bit and Grant leaned over my shoulder, watching. There was a squeak as Hannah's door opened on the screen and Kristen flipped on the light. Then, Hannah walked out in her pink pajamas.

"Hannah?" Kristen's voice shook. "Honey?"

The little girl turned, but her eyes were blank.

"Is she sleepwalking?" Grant asked.

I nodded my head. "I think so."

The frame shook as Kristen walked up the hallway toward her little girl.

"Hannah, it's bedtime, sweetie. Come on."

The little girl turned away and started walking toward the stairs. "I'm coming," she said. "Wait for me!"

Kristen grabbed the little girl by the arm and pulled her back from the stairs. The screen caught movement on the stairs, and the camera shook. The doll's cracked face appeared above the top stair. It stared at them, and then its body crawled up and it was in the hallway.

"Dalton!" Kristen shouted as she backed away from the doll, Hannah in tow.

The lights flickered in the hallway and then went out. Kristen screamed. A second later, the lights came back on. The doll was several feet closer, its limbs moving it down the hallway toward them like a broken spider. Another scream from Kristen and the slam of a door and the screen went blank.

I looked up at Grant.

"I would've left, too."

CHAPTER 19

"I don't think Amalie's family is here either," I said.

"Should I know what you're talking about?" Grant asked, his eyes searching mine.

"Give me a minute." I darted out of her room and almost ran into Mr. Brown and Tristan.

"Not a soul up here," Mr. Brown said. "They left every single light and television on in the house," he said, shaking his head. "Can't imagine why they left in such a hurry."

I can.

"Well, we sure appreciate your help tonight, Mr. Brown. You and grandpa got a Bingo night set up pretty soon?"

I caught Tristan's eye as he passed and he nodded.

"Yeah, we're headed over to the VFW Hall next week." He chattered on about the big game as he walked to the front door. Evie and Andy were there, talking with Mrs. Brown. They turned as we came downstairs.

I stood at the back of the group as everyone talked, moving slowly out to the front porch. Now that the threat had been nullified, Mr. Brown didn't seem in any hurry to leave. I turned and looked back at the kitchen. *Nothing. No fire. No screaming. Where are they?*

"Come on, Anderson," Andy said from the doorway.

I followed him out to the porch. Mrs. Brown locked the deadbolt behind us.

"Thanks for your help tonight," Tristan said as he shook the old man's hand.

I stepped down from the porch and walked around the corner of the house. I thought I heard laughter from the backyard and my arms broke out in gooseflesh.

Evie watched me.

I pointed to the backyard as we walked. "Do you get anything from back there?"

She tilted her head. "Something, but it's muted. I don't know what's back there."

Mr. and Mrs. Brown climbed back into his truck and he started the engine. "Tell your parents hey for me," he said to Tristan.

"Sure thing, Mr. Brown."

We watched as they drove out and pulled into the driveway down the road to return the key.

"Take the cars down the road," I said, tossing my keys to Tristan. "I have to check out the backyard."

Tristan and Andy got into the truck and my car and pulled out, heading along the road in front of the house. Evie, Grant, and I stepped into the shadow of the shed and watched as the Browns' truck passed by. They didn't slow down and their red taillights disappeared a few moments later.

"Come on," I said, walking toward the backyard.

"I don't get it," Evie said as she walked with me toward the backyard.

"You don't get anything here, which means that they're not in distress anymore. And, if they were still here, I would have been able to see the house burning."

"Oh," Evie said.

"Oh," Grant said.

We turned to look at him and he shrugged.

"The last time we were here, St. Louis saw a vision of the family that built the house. There was a mom, a dad, a boy, and a girl, Amalie. One night, the house caught on fire and the little boy died in the kitchen. The mother and father tried to extinguish the fire with buckets of snow, but they weren't able to put it out. They thought the little girl was trapped inside and they went to the front of the house when the fire got too intense back here. Amalie made it out, but she got turned around and she froze to death in the forest. We found her bones and they buried her next to her parents and brother. We thought we helped them, but then Kristen sent us a picture of the doll back here at the house."

"We saw," Grant started.

I shook my head at him. *If he tells Evie about the doll moving, she'll leave.*

Andy and Tristan came up the driveway and I handed them my phone. They watched the video as I walked into the backyard, Evie and Grant at my side.

The backyard was completely empty. I felt a cold chill winding its way up through me and I shivered. Glancing behind me, I scanned the quiet house. I sidled up to Andy and whispered, "Someone or some*thing* is watching us."

He nodded and got his camera out. He started filming as we walked back into the woods.

"Where are we going?" Grant asked.

"To where she died."

"Oh. Okay. That sounds…macabre. Terrible. Like the worst idea ever."

"You can wait in the truck," Andy offered as he handed my phone back to me.

Grant shook his head. "I'm fine. Is this safe?"

"Oh!" I texted my dad. *We're fine.*

He texted back that he wanted us home soon. In one piece, he added.

We followed the wind through the trees. In some places, it pushed us along, stinging our eyes as we walked. The darkness pressed in on us like a physical presence and the group got closer together the further into the woods we walked. When we got to the place where Amalie died, I stopped and took a sharp breath in.

"Look." I pointed. My gloved hand jutted out to a place on the ground near where her bones had been buried.

Evie gasped and Andy swung his camera around.

"Get me some more light on that," he said.

Tristan aimed his flashlight at the ground.

Near the place that had been disturbed recently when the little girl's bones were dug up, there was a smooth place cleared. It was roughly the size of a kitchen table and was completely cleared of leaves and sticks. Around the blank ground, there were the charred remnants of a circle made of rocks and sticks. Andy crept closer, narrating as he did so.

"What is that?" Grant asked.

"We think the ghosts are building portals." Tristan shuddered.

"To where?"

"We don't know." I took a step back and looked around the woods. I couldn't shake the feeling that something was watching, just beyond the reach of the light our flashlights made. Something rustled in the trees and I thought I heard laughter again. "Do you hear that?"

Everyone froze and stood listening. The wind picked up again and blew the iciness around us.

"I don't hear anything but the..." Andy started. Then, he stopped and cocked his head to the side. "I hear something."

"I hear it, too," Evie said. She took a step closer to me and wound her arm through mine. "What *is* that?"

Tristan pointed. "It's coming from over there."

I started walking toward the tree he pointed at, but Evie pulled me back.

"Nope," she said.

"We'll go together." I put my flashlight out in front of me and took one step and then another. The wind whipped my hair around my face as we walked. Grant and Tristan fell in behind and Andy brought up the rear. As we neared the tree, there was the sound of rustling and then the sound I had previously thought was laughter came through more clearly this time. This time,

I listened carefully and realized that it wasn't laughing. Something out here in the woods was crying.

"Amalie?" I said. "It's Marissa and Evie. Please come out. We want to talk to you."

The sound stopped and the wind died down suddenly, my hair floating on its last gasp. The entire area fell silent. I had to remind myself to breathe as we stood there, all of our flashlights aimed at the large tree trunk in front of us.

I slid my arm from Evie's and took another step forward. "It's okay, Amalie."

Evie's voice came from right behind me. "Amalie, remember me? I came to help you find your doll." Her voice caught in her throat as something stepped out from behind the tree.

I slid the beam of light to the right side of the tree and two eyes stared back at me. They were blue and glassy. It took me a second to wrap my brain around what I was seeing. When I did, I backpedaled, nearly dropping my flashlight as I collided with Grant.

"Please tell me you can see that?" I whispered. I glanced back and watched as Grant nodded his head up and down once, his eyes never leaving the tree.

The doll moved out from the shadow of the tree. Its face had cracked in several places and the hair was matted to its head. Mud and dirt were caked on the ripped dress and the limbs of the doll hung at odd angles. Its head lolled to the side and then snapped up as it took a step toward us, its legs bending at unnatural angles.

I stood frozen to the spot, leaning back against Grant for strength.

The doll moved again, its left leg dragging lazily through the underbrush, snagging as it moved. Its eyes never left me and it was scowling as it approached.

From the corner of my eye, I caught movement. Evie leaned down and grabbed a rock from the ground. She cocked her arm back, her eyes wild and her lips pressed together with determination.

"No, Evie!" I lunged toward her, but I was too late.

She hurled the rock directly at the doll. I watched it arc in the air, its mark true. It hit the doll directly in the face. There was a sickening sound of breaking porcelain like a gunshot in the quiet night. The doll's face splintered and a large chunk of cheek fell off, landing on the ground at the doll's feet. The doll rolled its eyes to look at me and then it fell to the ground, limp, its legs and arms splayed in broken angles.

I ran to the doll, my heart beating somewhere in my throat. It lay staring up at the night sky, exactly as Amalie laid so many years before. There was nothing in its eyes anymore. They were blank and empty.

I looked up. "You had no right to do that! It was her doll!"

Evie stood, her arm still in the motion of the throw. She shook her head. "I'm sorry, but that thing was coming toward us! Didn't you see how it was looking at you?"

The sound of cracking glass made me look back down at the doll. As I watched, the dress turned to threads and fell away completely, and then, the fabric that held the body together disintegrated, the stuffing inside turning to an ash-like substance that floated away on the night air. All that remained were the porcelain hands, feet, and head. The head lost its shine and one of the eyes broke into a million shards, falling down into the hollow head. It turned old right before my eyes and no longer resembled a doll, but a forgotten fragment of a child's plaything that had gone unused for close to two hundred years.

Tears clouded my vision.

"I'm sorry, St. Louis, I-I…" Evie stopped, a strange look taking over her features.

"What's wrong?" I asked a moment before I felt a pull on my energy. Something else was here.

"There's a disturbance now. A black color is hovering around the doll."

I turned to look and came face to face with a little boy. His skin was black and charred. Angry red lines covered his head and face where the skin had split, revealing the muscle beneath. His hair was gone and his nose resembled a skeleton. I cried out and turned my eyes away, gulping down huge lungfuls of cold air, trying to keep my stomach from churning.

"What is it, Marissa?" Grant took my hand. "I'm right here. What can I do?"

I found strength flowing into me as he stood holding my hand. The draining feeling ebbed and I was able to get my body under control. I swallowed.

"There's a spirit here," I said. I turned to look at the little boy. I took a deep breath. "Hans?"

He stared out from deep sockets, his brown eyes watchful, wary.

"Ja, ich bin Hans. Du hast meine Schwester genomen."

CHAPTER 20

I stood staring at Hans' spirit. A black cloud clung to his feet and I felt my insides crack.

"Hans, can you understand me?"

He tilted his head toward me, a few ashes falling from his head as he did so. "Yes, I go to school five years before I die."

"Hans, why were you in the doll?"

He looked down at the cracked toy at his feet. "I come to Amalie after we die. Amalie was scared of me. Amalie runned away." He turned his eyes toward me as I knelt down near him. "Are you not scared?"

I shook my head slowly. "No, Hans, I'm not scared of you. Your sister was only scared of you because she was just a little girl."

He pushed his jaw out in a defiant gesture. "*I* know that. I did not want her to be scared of me, so I made myself go into the doll. Amalie loved it so. We play together all the time then. Amalie and I."

"He was in the doll because he didn't want to scare his little sister," I said to the group.

"He was burned in a fire," Andy quietly explained to Grant.

"Hans, why did you try to scare the family that lived here?"

"The girl, Hannah," Hans spat, "I want her to go away. Let Amalie and me alone."

Realization and pity flooded my soul. "Hannah liked to play with you and she kept you away from your sister?"

"Yes, then you come with your friends, and now Amalie is not here and my parents," his eyes filled with tears, "they are not here anymore. You took me away and when I get back here, Amalie is gone. I am alone." His breath hitched in his little body.

"I am so sorry, Hans," I said. I turned to look at Evie. "I don't know what to do here."

Evie took a step closer and knelt down next to me. "We helped his parents move on when we reunited them at the gravesite. They left, but Amalie didn't. She was still here?"

I repeated her statement to Hans and he nodded.

"Amalie stand at the house and crying while you took me away. I walk for many miles to get back here. When I did, Hannah took me into her room and it was many hours until I could get to Amalie. By then, she was here. Amalie was talking to a man in the forest. He talked to her and before I could get here, a black smoke came up from the ground and...nahm, eh, took her."

"Sam," I breathed.

Evie's head snapped up and she looked at me.

"I think Sam took Amalie." I turned to Hans. "Did you hear what the man said to her?"

Hans' brow furrowed and he was quiet for a moment. "He talked to her in German. He said that our parents are with him. He said that Hans was with him. Lügner!"

"Sam told Amalie that he had her parents and Hans. She followed him through the portal. She must have felt so alone!" I felt my voice shift up an octave as my throat closed around my words. *I know how you felt, Amalie. I know what it feels like to be abandoned by someone you love.* "Hans, I need you to stay here. If that man comes back, you have to run the other way. Do you understand me? He is not a good person."

Concern took over Hans small features. "I take care of Amalie. Me. I take care of her."

Oh my gosh. "Hans, has the man already been here? Has he already talked to you?"

The black smoke thinned and then tightened around his ankles, snaking through the trees.

"Hans?"

He finally met my gaze. "He tell me I can be with Amalie. She miss me. Amalie needs me."

"No, Hans," I said, "you can't help her alone. This is too big for you to do alone."

"I take care of her," he said as he began to back away from me.

I tried to stand, but between the freezing temperature of the ground and the position I was kneeling in, my legs were all pins and needles. I pointed as Hans turned and ran, darting away from us between the trees, back toward his house.

"He's going that way! Don't let him go!"

Grant helped me up and I tested my legs. My head was swimming and I felt so ridiculously tired.

"We can't see him, St. Louis. You're the only one he can hear or see."

"Then what are we standing here for?" I took a step and immediately fell and hit the ground hard, twisting my leg as I did so. I cried out and tried to get up again.

Grant helped me, his eyes full of concern. Andy handed the camera to Tristan and grabbed my other arm.

He looked over at Grant. "You'll get used to this. At least she's light."

They draped my arms over their shoulders and held my waist as we made our way through the forest toward the house. The going was painfully slow and I gritted my teeth against the pain each time I put any weight on my left leg. As we finally got within eyesight of the house, I braced myself for what I would see. *Would Sam be there? Would he try to attack us again? Would Evie be able to hold him back this time?*

"I don't understand why we helped her parents move on, but not Hans or Amalie," Tristan said. "When we brought her body to the grave, if they moved on, she and her brother should have, too."

"St. Louis thinks something is keeping spirits here."

"Then, where are they?"

I shook my head. "I don't know."

"And, why didn't returning her body free her and her brother?"

"I don't know."

"And, why…"

I glanced back at Tristan. "Can we just assume that my answer is going to be 'I don't know' and move on?"

He narrowed his eyes then pulled out his phone and started swiping through the screen. Evie took his arm and guided him through the underbrush while he looked at his phone.

I peered ahead through the darkness, watching for any sign of Hans or Sam. My stomach plummeted when I thought of how scared and alone both he and Amalie had been. As we broke even with the tree line, I found nothing but the quiet still night surrounding the house. I looked over at Evie and she shook her head.

"Sorry, St. Louis, the disturbance disappeared while we were walking here. He's gone."

A strangled cry escaped my lips and I tried to pull away from Grant and Andy.

"Whoa, there. Maybe you should take it easy for, like, a minute?" Andy said.

"Marissa," Grant said, his voice warm near my ear.

I turned my head to look at him and my sight went dark around the edges. I felt my insides spin and then everything went muddy.

"Let's get her to the table there," Andy moved toward a picnic table in the backyard.

Evie ran over and cleared the snow from the seat with a gloved hand. Andy and Grant deposited me on the seat and I put my head into my hands, willing myself to stay awake. I closed my eyes and pressed the palms of my hands into them, welcoming the pressure that made the pounding in my head abate a small bit.

"Go get the car," Evie said. Keys clinked as they were tossed to someone. I didn't care who drove as long as it wasn't me, so I kept my eyes closed.

A brushing sound and then the seat creaked as someone sat down next to me. "You okay, St. Louis?"

I nodded, not moving my palms from my eye sockets. If I moved them, I swore that my eyeballs would fall right out.

"Has someone texted my dad lately?"

Evie reached into my coat pocket and pulled out my phone. A few seconds later, she put it back in my pocket. "Another half hour and all's well."

"All is *not* well," I snapped. "We've lost *another* ghost. Sam's out there collecting spirits for some reason. Grant's probably going to break up with me after this and my dad can see ghosts. How is any of this okay?"

Silence greeted my outburst and then Andy's voice. "Then, quit."

I moved my hands and waited for my vision to adjust, and then I looked up at him. He stood before me, his feet set wide apart in the snow and his eyes blazing.

"What are you talking about?"

"I'm talking about quitting. Listen, I'm sick to death of you pouting around and whining that you can't help anyone."

Tristan walked over and placed his hand on Andy's arm. "Andy," he said quietly.

Andy jerked his arm away. "No, she needs to hear this. She needs to know that she has helped more people than she has any idea. Mary, Theodore, Amalie,

Amalie's parents, Beth, Red," he ticked off his fingers as he talked. "You've helped the living, too. Melanie, your dad, Evie, me." He stopped and glared at me. "You help everyone you come into contact with, Marissa Anderson, because you try. You might not get it right every time, but you care and you give a voice to people. Do you know how *rare* that is?"

I glanced at Evie. She had her head lowered and was staring at her hands. Tristan stood looking off over the woods.

"I don't know what I'm doing," I said helplessly.

"None of us do!" Andy rubbed his hand over his mouth. "We don't know what we're doing, but we're trying."

"What if we're making it all worse?" I asked, my voice small as the headlights of my car swept into the backyard.

Grant got out of the car and strode over, stopping outside the circle we were in. "Everything okay?" he asked.

"Is it?" Andy challenged, looking right at me.

I met his gaze and took a deep breath. "Okay, we have to find out if Sam has taken anyone else. Andy, tomorrow morning, you and Tristan can go check the house at the Weeping Bridge. Take Evie. She'll be able to tell if anything's left making a disturbance. If there's not, we'll have our answer. Look for anything that looks like a portal. Take a picture of it. Grant and I will drive out to the Dietrich farm after I help my dad and Melanie. We'll meet back at my house and go from there."

Everyone was quiet for a moment. A slow smile spread across Andy's face. "There she is," he said.

CHAPTER 21

The ride back to my house was quiet. Grant concentrated on the road, following Andy's truck out to the main road. He flipped his lights as Andy headed one way toward home and we turned the other.

When we turned into my driveway, Grant drove to the back of the house near the shed and parked next to his car and Dad's truck. The back door of the car opened and Evie got out.

"I'll tell your dad we're home."

"Thanks," I mumbled as she closed the door and darted up the steps, eager to be out of the car, I thought.

When she was inside the house, Grant turned to face me across the center console. He held out my keys to me and dropped them into my hand. I put them in my coat pocket.

"So, that was a ghost hunt?" he asked. His eyebrows were lowered over his eyes and I couldn't quite read his emotion.

"Not really. You shouldn't have gone tonight."

"No!"

I looked up and he reached across the seat and grabbed my hands in his.

"Marissa, do you get what a cool gift you have? How much I love watching you do this?"

I shook my head. "I don't get how you aren't scared away by all of this. I mean, I would totally understand if you didn't want to hang anymore. This is pretty heavy stuff."

His eyes softened. "I want to know all of it. All of *you.*"

My heart skipped a beat and I allowed myself a small smile. "I don't know what will happen from here. It could get a lot worse, and," I chewed on my bottom lip, "I have a feeling that it probably will."

His thumb rubbed across the back of my hand and he brought my hand to his lips and kissed it. "I'll be here."

"No, you'll be in Kansas City at school." I felt myself putting up a wall. *I don't want you to get hurt.*

"I'll be here when you need me. Is that better?"

I pressed my lips together and nodded. Part of me wanted to push him away even further. He didn't ask to be part of this.

"Now," he opened his door, "can I walk you to your door and give you a kiss goodnight?" He smiled.

I got out, locking up my car and taking the arm he offered. I limped across the yard and he helped me up the steps to the porch.

I could hear my grandparents moving around beyond the back door. I sighed.

"What's wrong?"

I shook my head. "Another night, okay? I think you've had enough tonight."

He wrapped his arms around me and I breathed in his cologne. I closed my eyes as he kissed the top of my head. When he let me go, he held me at arm's length and stared into my eyes.

"I love you, Marissa."

"I love you, too," I breathed as he leaned forward and kissed me. Warmth swirled around me and I forgot about the ghosts, school, and being completely and utterly drained. I smiled as he pulled away, my lips still tingling from his touch.

"What time do you want me here in the morning?" he asked.

"I'm going to the lake with my dad and Melanie in the morning. I'll meet you here after that?"

"Text me," he said as he headed down the steps and got into his car.

I watched as it drove around the house and then I went in the back door.

Grandma and Grandpa sat at the table, eating breakfast and talking. My grandfather looked at my grandmother and he smiled, a tender moment that I felt guilty for watching.

"Hey, lover girl," Evie said, crossing in front of my grandparents and hopping up on the counter. "Your dad's fine. He's in the office working."

"Thanks," I said. I limped past her and grabbed a soda from the fridge. "I'm going to bed."

"We need to talk," she said, following me up the stairs.

"Give me a minute?" I asked, my words slurring with my exhaustion. The minute I saw my bed, every single muscle in my body cried out for sleep. I went into the bathroom and washed my face. The washcloth came away covered in dirt and makeup. I sighed and washed it out under the flow of warm water. Jerking a brush through my hair, I stripped out of my dirty, cold clothes and pulled on a warm pair of pajamas from the hook in the small closet. I grabbed a couple of aspirin from the medicine cabinet and swallowed them with a handful of cool water, hoping that they would take effect and calm the aching in my left leg before I went to sleep.

I opened the door and limped across my room, lifting the blanket and crawling underneath. Evie sat on the futon, her hair pulled up in a loose wet bun and a huge T shirt hanging from her shoulders. I tossed her a small blanket from the end of my bed and she caught it, wrapping it around her legs.

"How did you take a shower already?" I asked, scooting down until the comforter was wrapped up to my neck. The sheets below were deliciously cool and I focused on relaxing my muscles one at a time.

"I didn't want to be in your way," she said, shrugging. "I never want to be."

"What's that supposed to mean?" I asked. I was in no mood to decipher any of her crap tonight. I was too tired and too emotionally drained.

"I only meant that I felt like I was in the way the whole way home. Did you and Grant get a chance to talk?"

I nodded. "Yeah."

"He's sticking around, isn't he?"

"Yeah," I said again, rubbing my leg with my hand, urging the tight muscle to relax. "He's sticking around."

"I'm the one with the abandonment issues. Why are you so worried you're going to scare him away?"

I shrugged. "I-I don't know. It's a lot for someone to deal with."

"We all have our baggage."

"True." My phone buzzed on the nightstand. I picked it up and looked at the screen.

It was Grant. *I'm home. Are you sure you don't want me there with you in the morning?*

I chewed on my bottom lip.

"He loves you, like I love Sam."

My heart twisted and I texted him back. *Be here at 8:00.*

Night, my paranormal princess.

I snorted and texted him a heart emoji, and then placed my phone back on the nightstand.

"Evie, I'm really sorry about Sam. I can't imagine."

She pulled the blanket up around her neck. "It's okay. We're going to help him." Her voice was quiet. "I don't think he's so far gone, you know."

"I know." I thought about all of the times my best friend had been hurt by the people she loved.

Evie got up and stretched. She tossed the blanket back on the foot of my bed. "Night."

"Goodnight."

She started to leave.

"Evie? You should come with us, too, before you go out to the Weeping Bridge. I'm sure my dad will want you there."

She smiled. "Yeah, I'll come." She snapped the light off as she left my room.

I snuggled down into the covers and thought about Grant. His smile, his eyes, his kisses. I slipped into sleep thinking of the way he looked at me, like my grandpa looked at my grandma.

I dreamt that I was walking up to Mary's house. It was as it had been in the memory. Matthias and Mary sat on the sprawling porch, leaned back in wooden rocking chairs. Their happy voices carried on the spring breeze, punctuated with laughter. I walked up to the steps and stood, afraid to call attention to myself, afraid that any movement or sound I made would tear them from the happiness.

"Come with me," Matthias said. "You would love Carlisle. It is near Little Rock and I have a house there. It's not as spacious as this," he swept a hand at the mammoth two-story home, "but it is sturdy and warm."

"Culvers Grove is where I grew up," Mary responded. "It is my home. Not only this house, but this land, this town, they are all that I know."

Matthias reached out and took her hand. "You know me," he said, his eyes soft as he pulled her hand to his lips and kissed it.

"That I do," she said.

I smiled and they turned to look at me. The sun dipped behind a cloud and the day was plunged into a muted grayness. The wind picked up, tearing the flowering buds from the tree limbs. They scattered around me, enveloping me in the scent of happiness before they skittered away, lost in the encroaching forest.

Matthias stood up in front of Mary, his stance protective, watchful.

"What is it, dear?" Mary asked.

He scanned the yard, his eyes passing over me. Shaking his head, he sat down again. "I do not know. Something in the wind shifted." He placed his hand on Mary's as it rested on the armrest of her rocking chair, his eyes still watchful. "If we returned to my home, I would no longer be at risk of being recognized as a Confederate deserter. Word about town is that the war is almost over. We could live without the danger of having our secret discovered."

Mary seemed to think this over for a few minutes. She took a deep breath and looked deep in Matthias' eyes. "I will go with you. Let's leave this place when the summer arrives. The roads will be easier to traverse once the rain has abated. This house has never held any happiness for me," she blushed, "until recently."

Matthias smiled and kissed her hand again. "Then it is decided. We will leave when the summer arrives."

I felt a tug on my middle and the world spun around me. I was at a small country church. Several horses, wagons, and old cars were scattered around in the grassy field. The small whitewashed building with a simple box steeple at the top stood at the end of a small town, its yard flanked by a grove of trees. A cemetery abutted the back wall of the church. Voices carried out to me and I walked up the steps, pulling the door open. A dozen or so people sat in the pews, reciting a prayer together: "Denn dein ist das Reich und die Kraft und die Herrlichkeit in Ewigkeit. Amen." I watched as a younger version of Theodore Dietrich stood up as the congregation slowly exited the building. I followed him outside. A beautiful woman stood near a car, her parents talking with another couple from the church.

Theodore approached her. "Hello," he said, offering his hand.

The young woman blushed and took it. "Greta," she said.

"His wife," I whispered.

A cloud blew over the sun and an icy wind blew the young woman's skirt around her legs. She looked up at the sky.

"I wanted to welcome you to Culvers Grove," Theodore said. His hand continued to hold her hand as he spoke.

"We have felt so welcomed after moving from Wisconsin," she said. She dropped her head and gazed up at him through thick black lashes.

"If it pleases you, I would like to ask your father's permission to call on you sometime," Theodore said.

The tugging pulled at me again and I lost my breath as I was whirled around, spinning through darkness before being knocked into the bright light of a fall day on a college campus. I recognized it immediately as St. Louis University. Dad had taken me to look at it while I was growing up. I wasn't surprised to see a younger version of my dad walking along the pathway toward Dolphin Pond. His head was down and he was concentrating on the book in his hand while he walked. A woman with beautiful chestnut-colored hair stepped out into his path, and he tripped over her foot, his book flying. He recovered quickly and managed to stay upright, just barely though. I stifled a giggle. The day grew cold and I was quiet again.

I stood watching my dad and mom meet for the first time. She was visiting a friend on campus and they had been so enamored by each other that they became engaged at Christmas and were married by the next summer in her hometown of Troy. My heart hurt as I watched my mother, so full of life and happiness. They sat on a bench at the edge of the pond, talking and laughing in the sunlight as the stone dolphins spit streams of clear water across the pond at one another. My mom was so beautiful. She tucked her hair behind her ear in a motion that was so familiar that I gasped as if I'd been punched. It hurt all over again. Everything. I wanted to go and stay, all at the same time. My dad looked so happy. I wondered for a moment if he would have asked her out if he had known the heartbreak that would happen years later. Then I decided if he hadn't asked her out, he would have missed out on over twenty years of happiness.

They stood up and walked away, holding hands and talking with their heads close together. I swiped at my eyes and stood there, waiting for the tugging sensation to begin around my middle. It didn't come.

"Hey!" I shouted. "I'm ready to go now!" Nothing. I tried again. "What is this all about? Why show me this? I get it. I should allow him to love me. I get it, all right?"

I spun around, looking up at the sky. As I spun, the sky began to spin the opposite way, creating a vortex that angled down at my forehead. I looked up through the vortex of spinning sky and clouds and squinted. There was something on the other side. It was dark, but light as well. I leaned toward it and the vortex caught me, urging me upward toward the tight circle of light and dark at the top. As I approached, I started moving faster, the wind knocked out of me as I ascended. At the top, the light and dark began to solidify into separate entities. The light had a lone figure, strong but weakening as I watched. The darkness was filled with several entities, milling around, crying out in agony, reaching out with straining arms toward the light. The circle snapped closed and the vortex was gone. I was falling, plummeting toward the earth. I put my hands up to break my fall and cried out.

I landed with a thump on the floor, my comforter tangled around my legs. Kicking at it, I managed to free myself from its grasp. I sat up, my back resting against the side of my bed, breathing hard and pulling the strands of my dream back from oblivion.

A light knock on my door and my dad peeked in. His face spread into a grin. "Who won?"

"What?"

"Looks like the comforter won that round."

I closed my eyes, trying to hang onto the last vestiges of the dream. "I had a bad dream. Or a good one." I opened my eyes. "It had both."

"Most do if you look hard enough. I'm going to make a pot of coffee. Why don't you come down and chat with me before she wakes up?" He nodded toward Evie's room.

"Um, okay," I said.

Dad started to close the door.

"Hey, Dad?"

"Yes?"

I cocked my head to the side. "I didn't know you were such a klutz when you and mom met."

He gave me a strange look. "Yeah, um, I was, I was pretty much a complete dork. I really lucked out with your mom." He smiled again, this one the sad and wistful one he saved for when he thought about my mom. "I'll see you downstairs?"

"Yeah, give me a few minutes." I checked my phone. It was only seven in the morning. I groaned and got up to make the bed. The dawn was breaking outside my window, everything outlined in gray. I thought about Grant and smiled. *Yeah, I love him.* I smiled again. *Then you should stop pushing him away.* "I know, I know," I muttered, heading into the bathroom to take a shower, the dream playing over and over in my mind.

CHAPTER 22

Thankfully, Dad was sitting in his office when I got downstairs. I grabbed a soda and granola bar from the kitchen, skirting around my grandma as she took the biscuits from the oven again. I peeled the foil from the granola and shoved half of it in my mouth, munching as I walked into the office and tucked myself into one of the leather chairs.

"Morning," I mumbled, cracking open my soda.

"Breakfast of champions," Dad smiled. He took a sip of coffee. "What I'd give for your metabolism."

"What's up?" I asked.

He sat back in his chair and pulled the framed photo of his friend and him from the surface of the desk. He sat staring at it for a minute and then looked up at me. "I feel like I owe you an explanation."

I furrowed my brow. "For what?"

"For why I kept my ability to see things a secret for so long."

"Oh, that." I ate the last bite of the granola bar and tossed the wrapper at his trashcan. I missed.

He grunted and bent down to pick it up and put it in the trashcan. "How long have you been seeing things?" he asked.

I shrugged. "All my life, I guess." I told him about the piano and about seeing the ball of glowing light in my grandma's basement. "I didn't see as many, though, until I moved here."

Dad regarded me for a moment. "I understand. Growing up here wasn't easy. I saw them all the time. It was strange and draining and I didn't have anyone I could talk to about it."

"What about your mom or dad?"

Dad shook his head. "Mom was worried someone would think I was addled in the head and Dad wouldn't hear of anything he couldn't see with his own eyes. You know why Missouri is called the Show-Me-State, right?"

"I read somewhere that a congressman from Missouri said in a debate that the other party would have to 'show him.'"

"Nope," Dad shook his head, "it's totally because of my dad."

"You're making that up."

Dad chuckled. "Has it been hard for you here?" he asked quietly.

I thought about the question for a minute. Then, I shook my head. "Some things have been harder than others, but I feel like I belong here. Something about this place..."

"You know you were born here, right?"

I froze. "Seriously? I always thought I was born in St. Louis."

Dad smiled. "That was the plan. Your mom was eight months pregnant and insisted that she come with me to help my father put all of his affairs in order when he found out he was sick. I planned to drive up and spend a couple of days and she didn't want to be alone that long. So, we rented a hotel room in Eagleton and headed up here. We were out at the farm and I was helping Dad with all the paperwork and your mom and grandma were out in the garden. Your mom came in and said she felt funny and ten minutes later, we were headed to the hospital in town. You came a few weeks early and we got to take you home to St. Louis."

I tilted my head. "Why didn't you ever tell me about that?"

He shrugged. "I don't know. It didn't seem important."

"So, since you're not making eye contact, I can only assume that you're not being completely honest with me?"

He narrowed his eyes. "Hey, that's my trick."

"Come on, spill it. Why didn't you tell me that?"

Dad sighed and tented his fingers on the desk. "I hated this place. I hated growing up alone. I hated that I lost my best friend here. I hated that I wasn't on speaking terms with my dad."

"You broke all ties with this place," I finished for him.

"Yeah, I guess I did."

"So, how's being back here for *you*?" I asked.

His lips twitched. "Easier than I thought it would be. You know I never planned that things would go like this, but now we're here."

"You can make things better," I said. "You can tell your parents the things you should have said while they were alive." My eyes darted to the kitchen.

His gaze followed mine. "Are they here? Marissa, do you see them here?"

I pressed my lips together. "They're in the kitchen."

Dad's eyes filled with tears and he let out a strangled noise. "Oh, Marissa, I didn't know."

"It's okay," I said quickly. "They're not really here. Um, they're like a memory. They replay a happy time over and over again."

"What's their happy time?" he asked. His voice was small and a quiet desperation reached out to me from his eyes.

I knew what he wanted me to say. He wanted their happy memory to be a time he spent with them. My heart twisted. I cleared my throat.

"They're, um, eating breakfast. They're old, like how I remember them when I saw them."

Dad took a deep breath. "I see." His tone hardened and he pushed his chair away from the desk. He walked past me and through the living room.

I got up and ran after him. "What are you doing?"

"You're right. I should have told them the things I needed to before they died."

"Wait, you can't," I said, grabbing his arm.

"I'm getting ready to go out and talk to the ghost of my best friend," he said. "If there's any time to see if my ability still works, it's now." His voice sounded scared.

"Dad, you can try to see them, but please, don't try to interact with them?" I pulled at the sleeve of his flannel shirt. "I've made that mistake."

"What do you mean?"

"Every time I try to touch a ghost or interact with one, they are pulled out of the happy memory they were replaying and they, they get angry and sad." I let go of my dad's shirt. "Do you remember what happened to Thomas when you shoved him?"

Dad nodded. "I remember."

"I'm sorry you have unfinished business with Grandma and Grandpa, but if you touch them, they'll be thrown out of this memory. They'll know that they're dead." Sadness crept into my voice. "They're so happy now," I whispered.

Dad closed his eyes and took a deep breath, his shoulders moving up with the motion. He shook his head. "You amaze me." He took a step forward. "Come on. I want to see if I can see them. I won't mess with them, I promise."

I watched as Dad stepped under the archway that separated the dining room from the kitchen. He looked back at me and I pointed to the counter where Grandma was cooking.

"She's making breakfast," I said.

Dad turned back to the kitchen and stood there, his body tense as he watched the counter. A few moments later, he shook his head. "It's not working."

I pulled a chair out from the dining room table and put it next to him. "Sit down," I said.

He sat.

"Now, the first thing I do is relax. Don't be so worried about if you'll see them or not. Then, I let everything, um, open up. I usually hear or smell something first. Then, I start to see them."

"Okay," Dad said. He closed his eyes and leaned back in the chair. "I'm relaxed."

"Do you smell the bacon? That's what I smelled first and how I found out they were here."

Dad's nostrils widened a couple of times. He shook his head. "I don't smell any..." he stopped talking and looked up at me with wide eyes. "Bacon and biscuits?"

I smiled. "Yes."

He closed his eyes again and he breathed deeply. "I can smell the lilacs from outside," he said. "They were my mom's favorite." He smiled again and opened his eyes. "Where is she?"

I pointed and he squinted.

"Can you see anything?" I asked.

"No, I can smell things, though."

"Maybe that's all you'll be able to do for a while," I said. "I mean, it's been turned off for a long time, right?"

Disappointment painted his features.

I put my hand on his shoulder. "I'll be there today. I'll be able to talk to Thomas."

"Morning, guys," Evie said. She skipped down the stairs and stopped a few from the bottom. Her eyes scanned my dad and a smile broke out on her face.

"What?" I asked.

"He's got the same colors around him that you do. Pretty cool, Mr. A." She walked into the kitchen and grabbed a cup of coffee and a banana from the bowl on the counter.

Gravel crunched on the driveway outside and I saw Grant's car pull up. *Crap.*

"Dad, I invited Grant to come along. I hope that's okay."

Dad stood up to put the chair back under the dining room table. He brushed a hand over his mouth. "If Melanie doesn't mind, I guess it's okay with me. I'll ask when I call." He left to go to his office and call Melanie.

Grant knocked at the back door and Evie let him in.

"Hey," he said as he walked over and kissed me on the forehead. "How's the leg?"

"Better this morning."

Dad came out of the office a minute later. "Melanie says she's waited more than twenty-five years for this. She said it's been a big week, ghostly speaking, for her. I'll take my truck. Genevieve, you can ride with me. Grant, you and Marissa can follow behind. We're going into town to pick Melanie up first."

"You ready?" Evie asked.

I grabbed my coat. "Yeah. Let's go help them."

We filed out the back door and headed to our cars.

Grant opened the door for me and I sat down, my mind swirling. He got in and turned on the car, turning the fan up. The hot air blew on me and I rubbed my hands together in front of the blower.

"Buckle up," Grant said. He backed up and followed Dad's truck out of the driveway.

As we pulled onto the main road, Grant shifted and reached over to hold my hand.

"How'd you sleep?" he asked.

"Good, I guess. I had a weird dream."

"Oh, yeah?"

"Yeah, I saw Mary and Matthias, and Theodore and Greta, and my mom and dad."

He glanced over at me. "Sounds interesting."

"I guess." I sat staring out the window. "So, when we get to town, I'm going to have to close my eyes, okay?"

"Um, okay. And, why?"

I told him about not being able to filter out all of the ghosts anymore and how it completely drained me.

"That sucks, Marissa."

Tears crept into my eyes. "I'm learning to deal with it."

"Why do you think things changed?"

"I don't know. Everything changed when I saw the dark and light in the basement of the courthouse."

"You couldn't see them all before?"

"No, only when they were in trouble. Now, I see every single ghost."

"Are there a lot of them?"

I nodded.

He squeezed my hand and followed my dad into town.

"Close your eyes. I'll be right here."

CHAPTER 23

We pulled up in front of Melanie's house. I snuck a look and saw that she was already coming out the front door as my dad climbed the steps to help her. They shuttled her into Dad's truck and I closed my eyes again as we started driving.

"Let me know when we get out to the country," I said. "It should be safe then."

It took about fifteen minutes to get out to the lake, but I wasn't sure. Time and distance were hard to gauge when your eyes were closed. Grant talked about school and how he wanted me to come visit soon.

"I think you can open your eyes now," he said finally. "We're out in the middle of nowhere."

I opened my eyes. Dad's truck threw up a huge cloud of dust as we drove down a deserted gravel road. The morning sunlight glinted off something up ahead.

"I think that's the lake," I said.

We crossed a bridge and Dad's truck slowed.

"This must be really rough on your dad," Grant said.

Worry knotted in my stomach. My phone buzzed.

I pulled it out and looked down. Evie. *I don't see a disturbance here. That's not good.*

"Crap," I said.

"What's up?"

"Evie doesn't see anything up here. No disturbance. I didn't even think of that!" I smacked a hand against my forehead. "He might not even be here."

"Where did he go? You don't think Sam got to him?" Grant said, voicing the thoughts that were running through my head.

I texted Evie back. *Are you sure?*

A moment later, *Yes.*

I dialed my dad and he picked up.

"Dad, this might not work today. I'm not sure Thomas is here."

"I wouldn't forget this place." Dad's voice was grim. The phone went dead and I looked at it, my middle filling with dread.

"You said that Sam was taking spirits that were in distress, right?"

"Yes."

"What if when your dad shoved Thomas, it threw him into distress?"

The implications of that settled in me.

Dad's truck slowed again and then pulled off into the snow alongside the road. Grant followed and parked. I jumped out and ran to my dad's truck. He was already getting out.

"Let me look, first. Please. Let me see if he's here, okay?"

Dad regarded me for a moment. "Okay, I'll stay in the truck with Melanie. Be careful."

I looked around him at Evie. She scooted out of the truck and stood beside Grant and me. Dad got back in and sat staring out the windshield at the lake. His face was strained.

"Do you think Sam took Thomas?" Evie asked.

"I don't know," I said grimly. "Let's go find out."

We walked through the deep snow along the road. It evened out and wasn't as deep as we approached the lake. The edges gleamed with a thin layer of ice. The middle of the lake wasn't frozen and it rippled gently in the breeze. The only sound was my dad's truck running. Something about the area seemed reverent and I took a deep breath as we got to the bank of the lake.

I looked back at the road and saw the curve on the other end. I pointed. "If he came around that curve, his car would have ended up going in about here," I used my finger to point out the path that I thought the car may have traveled. "Can you see anything yet?" I asked Evie.

She shook her head. "Not a thing. I'm sorry, St. Louis."

"I'm going to try to find him," I said. "Don't let me freak out my dad, okay?"

Evie and Grant nodded and stood directly behind me as I looked out over the lake and then closed my eyes. The sound of gravel churning and tires grappling for traction hit my ears and my eyes flew open. I turned to see a car heading right toward us.

"Look out!" I yelled, ducking out of the way.

"You're seeing something that happened in the past." Evie's voice was near my ear. "There's nothing here now."

I took a deep breath. The car lost control and traveled down the hill, grass smacking at the front grill. Thomas and my dad were inside, their mouths stretched in grimaces as Thomas tried to keep control of the car. Dad was reaching over to help with the wheel when the car hit the water.

"This is the place," I said as the car began to sink. I shook my head. "I don't want to see this," I said. The image changed and my dad was sitting on the bank,

Thomas beside him. Thomas' edges were blurred and I knew he was already a ghost. I watched as my dad talked to him and then got up and shoved him. As he did, a black mist spread up around Thomas. He stared at my dad and his mouth moved. My dad walked away and Thomas stood there as my dad got in his car and drove away.

"Don't leave me!" Thomas shouted after his car. He started to run up the bank, but he hit an invisible wall and was sent sprawling on the grass. He got up and hit at the wall over and over again. "Don't leave me alone!" he shouted, pacing along the perimeter set by the wall like a caged animal.

"You don't have to be alone," a voice said.

Thomas and I both turned around and I saw Sam. He was standing on the edge of the water, dressed in the same clothes he died in.

I shook my head. "He's not supposed to be here." *He didn't go into the darkness until we went into the basement. Thomas died over twenty years ago. This doesn't make sense.*

"Come," Sam said, "I'll help you." He held out his hand.

Thomas regarded Sam warily. "Who are you?" he asked.

Sam smiled. "Someone that wants to help. No one should be alone."

Thomas looked back at the road, the dust from my dad's retreating car settling on the grass and tree limbs. "He'll be back," he said, "I'm his best friend."

Sam's features darkened. "He won't be back. He's leaving for good."

Thomas stared at Sam. "What do I do?"

Sam smiled. "You make a circle on the ground."

"From what?"

"Whatever you want. Twigs, grass, parts of the car. Anything really."

Thomas reached down and grabbed at a strand of grass. It slipped right through his hands. "I can't pick it up."

"You'll get there. It takes concentration, and time."

"And when I build this circle, what will happen?"

"I'll come back and I'll help you."

The image faded and I gulped in a deep breath. My knees gave out and Grant slipped an arm around my middle.

"Easy does it," he said.

"Sam was here," I said, "a long time ago! Evie, he's been taking spirits for a long time!"

She furrowed her brow. "I don't understand."

"He's always been bad, Evie."

Her eyes hardened. "No, he wasn't bad when he was helping me. How could he have helped me if he was being used by the darkness?"

"I don't know."

She stepped forward, inches from my face. "It's not true. He's not like that. You go back in there and you find out that you're *wrong*!" Her lips pulled back from her teeth and she reached out and shoved me in the chest.

I went over easily, my muscles in spasm as I hit the ground.

"What the heck, Evie?" Grant said. He leaned over and helped me up.

The door opened and closed on my dad's truck. "Marissa, are you okay?"

"I'm fine, Dad! Stay with Melanie!"

The door opened and closed again. Evie stood looking down at me, her hands clenched in fists at her sides.

"It's not true," she said through clenched teeth.

"I'm only telling you what I saw. Jesus, Evie! What is your deal?"

Grant looked from Evie to me. "What did you see, Marissa?"

I stood up, brushing snow from my backside. The adrenaline shooting through me gave me strength, but I knew from previous experience that it would be short-lived and I would pay for it later. I told them what I saw in the vision. "Sam was here twenty-five years ago. He told Thomas that he knew a way to help and get him to people so that he wouldn't be alone anymore. Evie, it's the same thing he said to Beth and probably said to Amalie and Hans."

Evie started pacing, shaking her head. "No, not my Sam. It doesn't make sense. He wasn't in the darkness then."

"What if he was in the light?"

We both froze and turned to look at Grant.

"What did you say?"

"What if, back then, he was working for the light? You said that there were both light and dark down in the well. What if back then he was trying to help people?"

Evie's eyes filled with tears. "That's it! He was helping people - ghosts! Just like we are trying to do now."

Grant looked at me. "What do you think?"

I closed my eyes and tried to focus in on Sam's essence in the vision. He *had* been different from the night out at the site of the wreck. There, he was like a wild animal, full of pain and rage. Twenty-five years ago, he had been calm, almost happy. I shook my head.

"I guess it's possible."

"Come on," Grant said. "Those two are probably up there having kittens."

"What are you going to tell him?" Evie asked.

I sighed. "I don't know. His friend isn't here anymore."

"Can you see more?" Evie asked. "I mean, can you see when Thomas went through the portal?"

I stopped walking and looked back at the lake. "I can try, but I'm almost out of energy now. I don't want to pass out in front of my dad and Melanie. It'll scare them."

"Okay," Grant said, "here's what we're going to do. I'm going to text Andy and Tristan and tell them to get out here. They can link with my phone for directions, then we're going to tell your dad that you can't find Thomas. Maybe he's moved on."

"He won't believe that."

"Then, I'll tell him that we think he should take Melanie home and then we'll meet him at the house once we find out where Thomas is."

"He won't go for that either."

"Well, then what do we tell him?"

"We lie. We tell him that Thomas is here and that he wants to tell Melanie something."

Grant furrowed his brow. "That doesn't seem right."

"If he's gone, if he's followed Sam into the darkness…"

Evie cleared her throat.

"Or the light," I said, "then he's not coming back here. No matter what I say, he's gone. My dad can't see ghosts anymore and Melanie never could, so the only one that could possibly see him is me. We'll tell them that Thomas has a message to pass along to them and then we'll tell them that I watched him go toward the light. We'll tell them that he's happy and safe."

"This doesn't feel right," Grant said.

"I know, but I think it's the only way. Besides, what are they both looking for?"

"Closure," Evie said. "They want to know that he's okay."

"We can't help Thomas anymore," I said, "but, we can help them." I nodded my head toward the truck.

Grant took a deep breath. "Okay."

He motioned for Dad and Melanie to come over and my dad helped the old woman out of the truck and through the snow to the bank of the lake. Melanie stood looking out over the water that had grown still. It was like glass under the mid-morning sun.

"It's so beautiful out here," she said quietly. She turned to look at me, her eyes full of tears. "He died in such a beautiful place."

Dad stood beside her, his hand on her arm. "I tried to tell you this years ago, Mrs. Ingalls, but I saw your son after the wreck. He used to sit here and look out over the water. He was quiet, calm, and happy. He said one thing over and over: 'Tell my mom that I love her.' I tried to come tell you that, but," his voice caught and he swallowed, his Adam's apple moving up and down in his throat, "the day your son died, he was trying to help me out of the car. He would have made it out if he hadn't stopped to help me out of my seatbelt." He took a shaky breath. "I am so sorry."

Melanie turned to look at my dad, her eyes full of tears. "Johnny, I never blamed you. I was angry and hurt that my son was gone, but I pushed you away, and in the process, not only lost my son, but a boy that I also thought of as a son. I am so sorry I pushed you away all those years ago. You didn't deserve that."

My dad's eyes filled with tears and he took off his glasses and wiped his eyes with the arm of his coat. My throat constricted and I leaned against Grant. Evie watched with a still face.

"You're not to blame for his death, you know," Melanie said quietly. "I know you've been carrying that around for half your life. It was an accident."

My dad's breath hitched in his chest and he put his glasses back on. "He was trying to save me," he said.

"Like you did so many times for him before," she said quietly.

Dad turned to look at her.

"You saved his life, Johnny. Thomas was headed down the wrong path and you came along and were his friend. He was happy when he was with you. You saved each other." Her eyes never left my dad's face as she looked up at him. "Now, I've said my goodbyes and made my peace. I used to be so upset that I couldn't bury my son, but now that I know that he is here in this beautiful place, I feel at peace." She turned to look at me. "Thank you."

I nodded, afraid that I would start sobbing if I opened my mouth.

Melanie pulled her hat down on her head and smiled. "Let's go, Johnny. We'll stop at the diner and grab some biscuits and gravy and talk. We have a lot to catch up on."

Dad's chin quivered as his eyes met mine. "Thank you," he whispered.

I smiled and held onto Grant, fighting against my heavy eyelids.

"We'll be home a little later," Evie said. "Andy and Tristan are meeting us there."

"Okay," he said.

I watched as he helped Mrs. Ingalls up the embankment and back into the truck. He started the engine and turned around in the road, waving as he drove away.

As soon as he was out of sight, Grant and Evie carried me up to his car and helped me into the backseat. He started it and warm air blew over my tired eyes. "Just a quick nap," I said.

CHAPTER 24

I woke up, my eyes adjusting quickly to the bright sunlight streaming in through the car windows. I sat up and stretched, my body hurting all over.

"Morning, sunshine," Grant said from the front seat.

"Hey." My mouth was dry and I licked my lips.

"Here," Grant said, handing a bottle of water back to me.

I took it gratefully and gulped down half of it in one swallow.

"Andy and Tristan are here. They took Evie and went out to Mary's and then swung by the Dietrich farm."

I stared at him, clenching and unclenching my fists, trying to get the circulation to start up in my hands again. "How long was I out?"

"About three hours."

"You stayed here the whole time?"

He smiled, his arm thrown over the seat and turned around looking at me. "Of course. You're pretty cute when you sleep."

I felt heat creep up my neck and onto my cheeks. *I hope I didn't snore.* I glanced down to make sure I hadn't drooled on his seat.

"You didn't snore or drool," he said.

"What did they find out there?" I asked.

The door opened and Evie scooted into the passenger seat. "We saw your head pop up. Glad to know you're with us again."

"Did anyone text my dad?"

"I let him know that we were going to grab lunch and then head back to the house," Grant said. "That should buy us another hour."

"Thanks." I looked at Evie. "So, what did you guys find out there?"

"Well, we went out to Mary's and there was no disturbance. The bridge is completely washed away now, but we could see what used to be a circle on the opposite bank. She's gone."

Crap.

"What about Old Man Dietrich?"

That was a little trickier. There's a family living there now, but I didn't see a disturbance over there either. I was able to make it upstairs to use their restroom and I peeked into the room that we found him in. It's been turned into a playroom for the kids and I saw what used to be a circle of cars on the carpet."

Double crap. Sam has so many of them now.

"What is he doing with the spirits he's taking?" Grant asked.

"I don't know."

"It can't be good, though," Evie said.

The back doors of the car opened and Andy slid in on my right and Tristan on my left.

"Hey, Anderson. Patton fill you in?"

"Yeah," I said. "Sam's taken them all."

"She told us that you saw him take someone, like, twenty-five years ago?"

"Sam was here. He told Thomas that he didn't have to be alone anymore. He told him how to build a portal and said that he could help him." I chewed on my thumbnail. "Grant thinks maybe he was working for the light before. Evie wants me to see if I can watch when Thomas goes through the portal."

"You feeling up to it?" Andy asked.

"Do you need food? Here," Tristan said. He handed me a package of beef jerky and a candy bar.

"Thanks." I took the food and nibbled at the edge of a piece of jerky. It was salty and absolutely delicious.

"Seriously, Anderson, I have to teach you how to eat." Andy grabbed a huge piece and shoved it in his mouth. "You ready?"

I nodded and tore off a big piece of jerky, chewing it as we all piled out of Grant's car and headed down to the lake.

"Okay," I said, "I'm going to try to concentrate on pulling up the memory of when Thomas left." Somehow saying it out loud helped me focus. I closed my eyes and focused in on the feeling around the area. I walked a few steps forward and looked down. A circle of twigs and leaves was at my feet. "It's here," I said.

The sun shone down and I felt heat rising up off the water. A thin film covered the water and mosquitoes buzzed around a spot near the shore. Cicadas droned on and the air was hot in my lungs.

"It's summer," I said. "Hot."

"What do you see?"

I turned around, looking for Thomas. He was up near the road, sitting on the embankment, looking down at the lake. I followed his gaze and watched as the water churned. A moment later, Sam's head broke the surface and then he stepped up and out onto the bank.

"Thomas," he said by way of greeting as he made his way up the hill through the long grass. It swished around him.

"Will it hurt?" Thomas asked, as Sam sat down next to him.

Sam laughed and then turned to look at Thomas. "And people call me a chicken. Of course not. This is a good thing, Thomas. You'll be with people again. You'll be so happy that you'll forget everything bad that ever happened to you."

"Will I forget about everything?"

"Yes."

"I'll forget about the accident and the sadness?"

"Yes."

Thomas squinted against the sun's bright rays playing on the water. "Will I forget the good things?" he whispered.

Sam threw his head back and laughed again. "How could you be happy if you forgot all of the good things?"

Thomas looked over at Sam. "Why are you doing this?"

Sam took his hat off and held it in his hands, regarding it carefully. When he spoke, his voice was full of emotion. "No one should ever feel like they're alone. I might not be able to do much, but I can help in this small way."

"What do I need to do?"

"First, you need to shed that." Sam motioned at the black mist swirling around Thomas' ankles.

I took a step closer. "Thomas has a black mist around his feet. Sam told him he needs to get rid of it."

"How do I do that?" Thomas asked.

"Forgiveness."

"I don't understand."

"You have to forgive to move on with me," Sam said, squinting out over the water.

"I don't have anyone to forgive."

"You don't?" Sam stood up. "Well, I guess my job here is done." He started to walk away. "But if that were true, you wouldn't have that mist around you."

"Wait!" Thomas stood up. "I-I don't know who to forgive."

Sam stopped and looked out at the water again.

Thomas froze. "I forgave my friend, Johnny, a long time ago. It wasn't his fault that I died. He tried to save me. I watched him swim down over and over again. It was my fault that we had the wreck. Not his."

Look inward.

I jumped when Sam's voice sounded in my head. I spun around and saw him standing on the bank, a smile playing on his lips.

Thomas looked up, his mouth open. "I have to forgive myself?"

Sam's smile spread. *Now you've got it.*

Thomas' eyes filled with tears and he closed his eyes, a tear running down his cheek when he did. He took a deep breath and a lightness took over his body. The black mist boiled at his feet and then latched on with tenacity.

You have to mean it.

I wasn't sure if that came from Sam or from me. I shook my head.

Thomas gritted his teeth and the black mist shattered, spreading out across the water like shards of glass. The shards sank with a sizzle and were gone.

There, that wasn't so hard, was it?

Thomas opened his eyes and smiled.

Now, step into the circle and repeat after me.

I shook my head again.

"What's wrong with her?"

"I don't know. St. Louis? Are you okay?"

Yes. No. Maybe. I don't know.

My head was spinning and my stomach lurched. I felt myself going down, my muscles tightening painfully. I focused on the vision in front of me. I wasn't about to leave here without seeing Thomas go into the portal.

Both Sam and Thomas were chanting something quietly and Sam came over to stand, his toes touching the edge of the circle. Thomas walked over, his legs stiff. He took one last look around and then stepped into the circle.

As soon as he did, a bright white light shot up, lighting up the entire bank in a shimmery brightness so jolting that I had to shut my eyes and look away.

Welcome home. It's all okay now.

I opened my eyes and watched as Thomas changed. He was no longer the pale drowned ghost I saw after Dad touched him, but a young man, full of life and laughter. He threw his head back and laughed, the sound resounding along the banks of the lake. A flock of birds startled and rose into the sky. The light intensified, burning my retinas and then, a sound like a jet engine roaring hurt my ears and then silence. The bank was quiet and still.

I opened my eyes and saw Sam standing at the edge of the circle. His face was stretched in a silent scream and his eyes bore into me.

Gisa!

CHAPTER 25

"Seriously?" I asked, sitting up in my bed and reaching for the glass of ice water someone had placed on my nightstand.

Tristan chuckled. "We got you home safe. Even made it past your dad without him seeing you."

I wiped at my mouth with the back of my hand. "What time is it?"

"Around three."

"Where's Evie?"

"Right here, St. Louis," she said, walking into my room through the bathroom. "What's up?"

I threw my legs over the side of the bed and faced her, throwing the comforter to the side.

"Evie, Grant was right, Sam was taking people into the light."

She sat down beside me. "Like, heaven?"

I shook my head. "I don't know. I didn't see anything after Thomas was engulfed in light." *Except Sam screaming.* I shook my head, clearing it. "I think he was helping Thomas."

"I don't think he was helping Red," Tristan said from his spot on the futon.

"I don't think so either. I think, even if he was helping spirits before, something changed."

"What?" Grant asked.

I pressed my lips together and swallowed. "Evie, what if telling us what happened while you were in the darkness is the only way to help Sam?"

The room grew quiet as we all stared at Evie. She blinked rapidly, tears spilling out of her eyes as she did so. Grant walked across the room and handed her his handkerchief. She took it and wiped at her eyes. Looking up, she set her jaw and took a deep breath.

"I don't have many happy memories," she said.

"Understatement of the year," Andy said.

Tristan nudged him.

"Sorry."

"But one of the best memories I have is when you and your dad helped me move out of my mom's trailer."

I felt the pressure of sadness crush my insides. *That's her happiest memory?* "Oh, Evie, that was such a terrible day."

She smiled through her tears. "No, it wasn't. I finally felt safe and like someone was in my corner. I felt like a part of a real family." She sniffed and wiped away more tears. "When I was down in the basement of the courthouse, being held by that *thing*, every single awful memory played through my mind over and over on a continuous loop. My mom hitting me. Her boyfriends touching me. My dad leaving. The kids at school making fun of me."

The muscle in Andy's jaw worked and Tristan placed a calming hand on his arm.

Evie went on. "I tried to think of a happy memory, something to make the pain stop. I thought about you and your dad driving me to my mom's trailer and packing up all of my stuff. I remembered getting back in the truck with you and feeling so happy. That it was all finally over, you know? I held onto that memory and pretty soon it drove out all of the other bad ones and I didn't feel so lost anymore." She took a deep hitching breath. "I don't think I can talk about this." She stared at me and I held her gaze.

"It's okay, Evie. You can tell us. You're safe here."

She nodded then looked down at her hands again. "The memory changed then. We were in the trailer and you were helping me pack things up in my room. Your dad came in and...and..." She took a breath. "He told you to come with him. You were leaving." Her voice broke. "He looked at me and said that he didn't want me to ruin your lives like I had ruined mine." Her voice broke as a sob wrenched its way from her core. She took a deep breath. "Your dad put his arm around you and you walked out the front door. I tried to talk to you, but I could only see the back of your head. I kept running around you and all I could see was the back of your head. You pushed me away and I fell. I was lying on the ground bleeding, and you and your dad got in the truck and as soon as you closed the doors, the truck blew up."

I gasped.

She glanced up at me and then back down at her hands. "I tried to get to you, but the truck was full of flames and you were screaming and your dad was burning."

"Oh, Evie. That's awful." I lowered my voice. "But, it wasn't real."

"That's the thing," she said. "At first I knew it wasn't real, but it replayed over and over so many times that I began to believe that it *was* real. It was the only thing I could see or think about. It was my reality, but then, I heard a whisper. A hissing, really. It told me that I could make it stop. All I had to do was give up. Let everything go and it would all go away." She bit her bottom lip. "The next thing I knew, I was in the hospital room and I was staring at my body."

"Would you have done it?" I asked.

Her voice wavered. "I would have done *any*thing to make it stop," she said.

I reached over and put my arm around her shoulders. She leaned into my side. We sat in silence, allowing Evie's words to resonate.

"And you think Sam is going through the same thing?" Andy asked her.

"I think that he was forced to make a choice to make it all stop."

"Now he's playing for the away team," he said.

"Both Red and Beth said the same thing to me," I said quietly. I looked over at Grant.

He nodded. "Andy and Tristan told me everything that happened."

"They both said that someone came to them and told them to build the circle to make the pain stop," I said.

"Sam?" Tristan asked.

"I think so. If what happened to Evie happened to Sam, and he chose to make it stop, then he might be working for the darkness now." I swallowed.

The room was quiet.

"So, what do we do now?" Andy asked.

"We have to help him."

My statement was met with more silence.

"We don't have a choice. He would do it for us."

Andy stood up. "Are you sure about that, Anderson?"

I bristled. "Don't forget that without him, Evie wouldn't be here with us."

"Do we have to go back into the cave?" Tristan's voice was quiet.

"I don't see any other way," I said. "We have to get back to the basement of the courthouse."

Andy shook his head. "How do you suppose that's going to work? You couldn't even get *into* the courthouse. You think it's going to be easier for you at ground zero?"

"We have to do something! You have a better idea?"

That shut him up and he sat down again, the muscle in his jaw working.

"We have time before it gets dark," Evie offered.

I put on my boots and stood up. "I'm in. Who else?"

"Me." Tristan stood up and Andy followed suit.

"Your dad's not going to be okay with this," Grant said. He walked over and handed me my coat.

I slid into it. "Fine, he can come with us."

I headed downstairs, not sure if anyone would follow. I let out a breath when I heard several footsteps on the steps behind me.

"We're going to try to help Sam," I said, opening the door to my dad's office.

He looked up over his glasses at me. "This is the same Sam that hurt Genevieve?" His eyebrow ticked up a notch.

"When we met him, he wasn't violent. He would never have hurt Evie. In fact, he's the one that came up with the idea to help her get out of the coma."

Dad peered around me at the group standing in the doorway. He took a deep breath and pushed his chair away from the desk. With a grunt, he rose and grabbed his coffee cup. "I'm going to get a new cup of coffee. You have until I'm finished with it to convince me that you should be going anywhere to help this guy."

I widened my eyes at Evie as we passed. We went to the dining room while my dad got his cup of coffee. There were enough chairs for everyone and we all sat down, leaving a place at the head of the table for my dad. He came in a minute later, a steaming cup of coffee in his hand.

Sitting down, he looked across the table at all of us. "Okay, go." He took a sip.

"When Evie got in her accident, it was Sam that wanted to find a way to help us get her back into her body."

Dad pressed his lips together.

"He didn't know how to do it, though, so he said he had to ask someone," Andy said.

"And he went to a really old spirit that lives in the basement of the courthouse."

"That basement has been blocked off for years," Dad said.

"Right, which is why we had to go through the caves."

He stared at me for a moment, his eyes narrow behind his glasses.

I took a breath. "We had to go. Evie was dying because her spirit couldn't get back to her body in the hospital."

"Why not?" Dad's coffee sat forgotten on the table next to him.

"Sir, Sam didn't know it, but there were two spirits down there, a good one and a bad one." Tristan leaned up, his elbows resting on the table. "The bad one was holding her. And, to save Evie, Sam went into the darkness in her place."

"Now, he's in trouble and we need to help him."

Dad tented his fingers and pressed them under his chin. "Then, why did Sam hurt Genevieve?"

"I don't think it was him," Evie said quietly. Then, her voice gained strength. "I think he was trying to keep me away. I think that, even if he's being held by the darkness, some part of him is still there. The part that loves me."

I stared at her.

"Fine." Dad pushed his chair away from the table and stood.

"Fine what?" I asked.

He shook his head and looked at me. "Fine, you can go try to help Sam, but I'm going with you."

CHAPTER 26

We trudged through the snow into the forest behind the house. Andy and I led the way with Tristan and Grant behind. Evie walked with my dad.

"He took it pretty well," Andy said. "My parents would have lost their minds."

I glanced behind me. "I don't think much surprises him anymore since we moved here."

"What are we going to do when we get there?" Andy asked.

I shook my head. "I don't know. The markings you made the last time we were there should still be there. We can follow those."

"Are you going down in the well again?"

I shivered and my stomach churned. "We'll cross that bridge when we get there."

We walked in silence the rest of the way. The hole in the rock face was quiet and dark and we all stood in front of it, looking at it.

"Let me," Evie offered, stepping down the gulch to the opening. She looked back at me. "You're coming, right?"

No. I think I'm going to head back to the house, wrap up in a warm blanket, and watch some TV. I swallowed. "Yeah, right behind you."

She disappeared into the hole and I scrunched down, climbing in behind her. She made it into the large cavern and I slid in, my shoes sliding on the wet rocks. The cavern was dark beyond the reach of the light streaming in from the outside. I turned as the light faded and saw Andy crouched in the opening. He grunted as he moved his tall frame through the tight space. I reached back to help him as Evie began to walk into the cavern.

"Wait," I said over my shoulder, "I'll come with you."

The words barely left my mouth when the entire space filled up with a desolate feeling. A wind kicked up from the back of the cave. Andy and I froze.

A shadow darker than the rest of the cave crossed into the space.

"Evie! Stay back!" I let go of Andy's hand and moved to grab Evie's arm.

A shrieking sound built and I slammed my hands over my ears.

"What's going on down there?" My dad's voice echoed.

"Evie, come on!"

Evie moved ahead, her head leaning forward as she peered into the darkness. The shadow moved again.

"Sam?" she asked. "Is that you?"

The shadow grew and the darkness deepened.

"Evie?" I reached forward and got hold of her arm. "Evie, that's *not* Sam."

The darkness reached out, grasping her feet with black threads. Then, it drew up eight feet in the air above us and came rolling toward us. Andy stepped up beside me and grabbed Evie as well.

"Wait," she said quietly. "Sam, its Evie."

The darkness stopped moving toward us, the blackness swirling above our heads, ready to pounce. It hesitated.

She held up her hands and pushed them toward the smoke. It recoiled, jettisoning toward the back of the cave. Tristan, Grant, and my dad came in through the hole just as the darkness dove into the hole at the back of the cave. The ground shuddered and then rocks started falling in front of the hole.

"Get out now," my dad said.

Andy and Tristan climbed through the hole and then Dad pulled Evie back. He moved her into the hole and she climbed out. Dad looked back at Grant and he nodded. He climbed through the hole and Grant grabbed my arm and pulled. I stood rooted to the spot as large rocks fell, covering the hole. A gigantic boulder rocketed down to the floor, shattering and sending smaller rocks out like shrapnel.

"Time to go," Grant said. He pulled me with him through the hole and we landed on the other side, a cloud of dust shooting out of the opening behind us. The ground shook for a long time and then everything was still.

"Is everyone okay?" Dad asked. He looked around at the group of us.

"We're fine," I said as I stood up and dusted the dirt and snow from my pants.

Dad whirled around, his eyes blazing. "Fine? Were you just in there? Did you see what happened?"

"Dad," I started.

"No." He held his hand up. "This is *over*. No more caves. No more Sam. This is done."

His voice faded into the night. We stood in a semicircle with my dad in the middle.

"Mr. Anderson," Andy said, "we're okay, really."

"I understand that, but if that cave-in had happened two minutes later." He stopped and rubbed his hand over his eyes. He pulled a butterscotch candy from his pocket and unwrapped it. He tossed it into his mouth. "This is over. We are done. Sam might be in trouble, but you are *not* risking your life to help this guy. Do you understand me?"

My cheeks were hot despite the icy wind. My eyes filled with tears.

Dad took one more look at me and then turned, walking away through the trees toward home. Andy and Tristan followed, sullen and quiet. Grant looked at me and I shook my head. He turned to follow.

Evie slid her arm through mine. "Come on, St. Louis, it's okay, he's scared."

I sniffed and started walking. "Me, too."

The walk back to the house was completely silent. My dad hung his coat by the door. We stood at the back door, watching as he walked over and poured himself a hot cup of coffee. He turned to look at us.

"I think it's time for the party to be over. Andy, Tristan, Grant." He nodded at them.

"Yeah, I need to get some homework done," Tristan said. "Night, guys."

He and Andy left and Grant gave me a peck on the cheek. "I'll call you."

"Bye."

When they were gone, Dad stood in the space between the kitchen and the dining room. The overhead lights deepened the lines on his face. He looked tired and old. Taking a sip of coffee, he stood looking at us. Evie and I hung up our coats and stood next to each other in the kitchen. My grandma moved between us, serving breakfast to my grandfather.

"Girls, I don't want to have to say this again, so listen carefully. I am responsible for you and I am not allowing you to do something that will result in you getting hurt. It's over and I don't want to hear another word about Sam or ghosts or anything."

"But, you remembered," I said, my voice small.

He shook his head. "I went my entire adult life without allowing that part of myself to come out and I was fine. Now, you need to learn to do the same, Marissa."

"I can't turn it off!" I snapped.

His eyes narrowed. "This is not negotiable. You two are my family. I am here to protect you and I will do so."

"But Sam," I said.

"He is not family. We don't owe him anything. You can't save them, Marissa. It's over."

I stood there, the air around me snapping. I took a deep breath. "Fine, we're done." I passed by him, anger seething off both of us, meeting in the middle with an almost palpable wall.

He cleared his throat and opened his mouth as if he was going to say something else, but I turned and headed up the stairs. Evie followed me. I heard his heavy footsteps and then the office doors closed with a bang. I stomped into my room and circled it, shaking my head and clenching my fists. Evie came in, closing the door and then leaning against it, watching me.

"What right does he have to tell me to quit seeing things? It's not like I can just stop it. Poof, and it's gone."

She stared at me while I fumed. "Mine's leaving," she said quietly.

I stopped. "What do you mean?"

"I can't see the colors around you much anymore. They're so muted." She shrugged. "Sucks."

"Can you still see distortions?"

She crossed the room to sit on the futon. "Yeah, but they're not as clear."

"This whole thing sucks," I snarled, kicking off my boots. "He's never treated me like this." I sat down heavily on my bed.

"He's never been so scared of losing you," she said.

I glared at her. "Whose side are you on, anyway?"

"I'm on your side, but I understand that your dad's scared. Think about it. Have you ever seen him look like that before?"

"I get it. He looked like that when my mom was sick and when you were in the coma."

"Good, now quit whining and let's figure out how we're going to help Sam."

My phone buzzed in my pocket. Two messages. One was from Grant. He said he was sorry things went down like they did, but he wanted to meet tomorrow. He was heading back to school Sunday afternoon.

I texted back that I would text him in the morning.

The other message was from Tristan. My eyes snapped wide. "Listen to this. He thinks we should try to show Sam a true memory. One that shows that his daughter is okay. Would that work?"

Evie squinted. "Yeah, if I had been shown that you and your dad were okay, it would have bought me some time down there. How do we do it?"

I thought for a moment.

"We find Sarah's ghost and build a portal."

CHAPTER 27

We texted back and forth with Tristan for a couple of hours, and between all of us, we narrowed down the list of Sarahs that lived in Culvers Grove to three names that fit the timing to be Sam's daughter: Sarah McMillan, Sarah Henderson, and Sarah Clifton. No maiden names were listed for any of them, so we weren't sure which one had been a Johnson, but they were all born in the early 1900s and had lived in Culvers Grove all their lives. Tristan texted that he would work on finding addresses and we would meet to go investigate tomorrow morning.

That is, if your dad lets you out of the house, he texted.

Shut up, Andy, I texted back.

Heh. Night, Anderson.

Evie retreated to her room and I sat up, running through whatever history I could dig up about the town. It didn't surprise me that the information was lean, but it was frustrating all the same. I had given up and turned off my laptop when I heard my dad climbing the stairs. I stood up and opened my door. He looked down the hallway at me, his hand on the banister that surrounded the front stairs.

"Hey," he said.

"Hey."

We stood, the uncomfortable silence between us unfamiliar.

"I'm going to bed. I'll see you in the morning."

"Evie and I are meeting the guys for breakfast and then we're going to work on a research project."

"And, that's the truth?"

I swallowed. "You have to trust me."

"I used to be able to," he said. Then, he walked down the hallway to his room.

I sighed and headed back into my room. After a shower and drying my hair, I sat in my bed, my comforter pulled up over my legs. My nerves were on edge and I was still mad about my dad, and even though

I felt completely drained, I knew sleep would be evasive. I pulled my sketchbook from my backpack and opened it to a blank page. Placing the tip of the pencil on the paper, I closed my eyes and let my hand move.

Several minutes later, my hand stopped moving and I opened my eyes. On the paper was a drawing of a beautiful Victorian home, flanked by weeping willow trees. In the upstairs window, a young woman stood, a veil over her face and a bouquet of flowers in her hands.

I let the book slide to the floor and snuggled down under the covers. I went to sleep and didn't wake up until Evie shook me awake the next morning.

"Come on," she said, "it's late."

"What time is it?" I mumbled.

"Nearly ten. Come on. Get dressed."

I sat up but immediately slid back down under the covers. "I'm too tired."

"Whatever," she said, opening my closet door and rifling through the clothes hanging there. "You got, like, twelve hours of sleep. Here, put these on." She tossed a pair of jeans and a long-sleeved maroon shirt at me.

"Get out," I snarled from under the blanket.

Cold air invaded my space as she ripped the blanket back. "Tristan found addresses for them all. We need to get going. Now, get up!"

She headed out the door and I threw my jeans at it as she closed it behind her.

I called her every bad name I knew as I dragged myself off the bed and put on my clothes. When I got downstairs, I slumped into the couch and pulled the quilt over my legs. Dad was in the office working at his desk.

Evie came out of the kitchen and tossed me a granola bar. "Let's go."

"Ugh." I got up and threw the quilt to the side. "You suck, you know."

She smiled. "Bye, Mr. Anderson."

He came to the office door. "What time will you be back?"

I shrugged.

Evie looked between my dad and me. "Um, we should be back after lunch."

He went back into his office without a word.

I followed Evie through the kitchen and out the back door. I climbed in the passenger seat and buckled up while she scraped the ice off the windshield. Evie got in, rubbing her hands together in front of the vents.

"You ready?" she asked.

I shrugged again and buried my face in the collar of my coat.

"Well, cool. It's a good thing you're as good as your dad at the silent treatment."

I ignored her and closed my eyes, leaning my head against the seatbelt. The car began to move and I tried to catch a quick catnap before we got to town.

Andy and Tristan were waiting for us in front of a rundown house on the edge of town. It sat on the end of Baker Street, right before the road turned into the highway. They were parked on a side street. Evie pulled the car up behind them and I opened my eyes a bit. This far outside of the middle of town, I didn't see many people or ghosts out milling around. I nodded to her and then stepped out of the car.

Andy and Tristan met us at the back of his truck.

"Which one is this?"

"McMillan. Henderson lived near the square and Clifton lived on a farm a few miles away."

My phone buzzed. It was Grant. I texted him that I'd let him know where to meet us later.

"Do you see anything?" I asked Evie.

She shook her head, staring at the house. "No, wait. Maybe?" She rubbed her eyes and looked again. "It's getting harder to see. There could be something there."

"Does anyone live there now?" I asked.

"Family of four. Mom, Dad, and two little kids." Tristan checked his phone. "It's Sunday, so they may be at church."

"Let's hope," I mumbled, making my way up to the door. "Just get me in for a minute. I'll try to find her."

We stepped around broken plastic toys, their once brilliant red faded to pink by the relentless sun. The front porch was covered in trash. I rang the doorbell and waited, the group on the porch behind me. No one came to the door and the house was silent. I reached out and tried the door. Locked. *That's fine. Not really wanting to rack up a breaking and entering charge before noon.*

"Okay, I'm going to walk around the house and see what I can find." I skirted around the side of the porch and through the bushes to the backyard, watching in the windows for any sign of Sarah. As I came around the side of the house, I couldn't believe my luck. The winter day turned into summer and I saw a woman sitting on a stump in the yard, a child on her knee. Three more children ran around the yard, their feet bare and smiles on their faces. Their laughter filled the yard and I found myself smiling as I walked over to her. I stopped in front and peered at her face. She had wide set eyes and curly red hair. Freckles spotted her face and she spoke with an Irish accent as she told her son a story. I squinted at her. She didn't look like Sam at all, but I couldn't be sure, since I'd never seen pictures of Sam's wife. I sighed and looked back at the front of the house. *Maybe I should touch her and ask.* My fingers reached out to her shoulder, but stopped a moment before they made contact. *What if I pull her out of this happy memory? I can't do that again.* I stepped back, wrapping my arms around my chest as the summer day faded and winter cascaded down on me with an icy splash. The day dimmed and I shook my head, pushing the tiredness down as I walked back to the front of the house.

I met the group and shook my head. "This woman was Irish and had red hair and freckles. I don't think it's Sam's daughter."

"You didn't talk to her?" Andy asked.

"No, she was with her kids and she was happy."

I shivered and Evie put her arm around my shoulders.

"It's okay," she said, shooting a look at Andy. "We'll try Sarah Henderson."

We piled back into the cars and followed Andy and Tristan to the middle of town. As we approached the square, I could feel the pressure of a dozen or more spirits pressing down on me.

Evie glanced over. "Close your eyes, St. Louis."

I nodded and did as she suggested. The car drove a bit farther and then I felt it stop. I opened my eyes a tad and then slammed them shut again.

"Are you okay?"

"So…many…here," I managed. "Take my hand?"

"Yeah, sure." Evie got out of the car and then my door opened and she took my hand in hers. "This way. Watch the curb now."

I squinted through half-closed lids as we approached a neat two-story house on the corner of Grant and Main. We climbed the porch steps and stood in front of a massive red door. I rang the doorbell and could hear it echoing inside. A small white-haired woman peered at us through the glass sidelights, and then opened the door.

"My goodness!" She wrapped the crocheted shawl around her bony shoulders. "It's a cold one today, isn't it?"

"Yes, ma'am," I said. "My name is Marissa Anderson and I was wondering if I could ask you a few questions?"

She regarded me with watery eyes for a moment, and then ushered us in. "I'm Mrs. Smith. Come on in out of the cold."

We stood clumped together in a small foyer. The wood floors gleamed and a chandelier hung over the space that led to a staircase.

"You have a beautiful home," I said.

She smiled. "Thank you. My husband and I restored it when we bought it, well now, I'd say that was almost sixty years ago now." Her lips twitched as she smiled. "It's amazing how the time flies. He's been gone almost six years."

I caught movement out of the corner of my eye and saw a man working on the floor in the sitting room to my left. His hair was white and his hands were gnarled with arthritis, but he wore a smile while he worked. My dad had the same look when he was working on a case he loved. The old man was happy. Looking over at Evie, I raised my eyebrows. She peeked past me into the room and then shook her head.

"We were wondering if you could tell us anything about the people that owned the house before you," Tristan said.

"Come on in and sit down," she offered. "No sense in having you stand out here."

We followed her into the sitting room and I tried to peel my attention from the old man hammering on the floor.

"Would you young people like anything to drink? I think I have some apple juice and I could make a pot of hot chocolate."

"Thank you, Mrs. Smith. We only have a couple questions and then we'll get out of your hair."

She chuckled and sat down. "I don't get many visitors, especially ones famous like your friend, here." She nodded toward Evie.

"I-I'm sorry?" Evie said as she sat down.

"Oh, we were all rooting for you while you were in the hospital. We took up a collection at our church to help your mother with the hospital bills."

Evie's mouth drew into a thin line. "A collection? For my mom?"

"Well, yes, dear. We all help one another in a town like this."

I glanced over at Evie. Her face was gray. "Um, Mrs. Smith, about the previous owners?"

"Ah, yes. Henry and Sarah Henderson. They were quite old when we bought the property from them. As I remember, they were downsizing and moving into an assisted living community over in Bethany. This old house was too much for them and quite a mess when we moved in."

"They died in Bethany?"

"Well, I believe they did. We dealt with their daughter, Allison, mostly."

"Did she mention anything about Sarah's family?" Andy asked.

Mrs. Smith regarded him for a moment. "Not that I recall. Allison did mention that they immigrated to the states from Poland after they got married."

"So, they weren't from Culvers Grove?"

"No, I don't think so."

I used the moment that she was focused on Andy to put out some feelers. My attention was pulled to Mr. Smith as he worked near us. "Mrs. Smith, do you mind if I use your bathroom?" I asked.

"Sure," she said, "it's the first door on the left past the stairs."

"Thank you." I got up and headed down the hallway. I opened and closed the bathroom door and then went to the kitchen. I poked my head in and saw nothing.

Crossing back into the hallway, I caught Andy's gaze and moved my eyes to the ceiling.

"That's a really cool lamp," Andy said, pointing at a lamp to Mrs. Smith's right. She followed his gaze and I darted across the open space to the stairs, climbing them, hugging the wall so that they wouldn't creak. When I got upstairs, I was able to see in all of the rooms from the top. I did a quick mental sweep and then headed back down.

I opened and closed the bathroom door again and came back into the sitting room while Mrs. Smith was still telling Andy about the lamp. I sat down on the couch next to Evie and shook my head slightly.

"Mrs. Smith, we wanted to thank you for talking to us today, but we need to get back home. I promised my dad we'd be there to help him with chores."

She smiled. "Well, thank you for coming by to visit a lonely old woman." She stood up. "Hold on just a minute, I have something for you," she said to Evie. She disappeared into the dining room and opened the drawer on the sideboard. She came back with an envelope and handed it to Evie. "Now, what I didn't mention before is that while we help one another out in a small town like this, we also know who needs help and who doesn't." She placed her hand on top of Evie's and peered at her intently. "Am I correct in assuming that this money would be better put to college rather than helping to support the local bars?"

Evie gaped at her.

"That's what I thought," the woman said. "I was going to drive out to give this to Mr. Anderson since you are staying with him, but this saves me the trip. Use it wisely, young lady."

"Um, y-yes, ma'am," Evie managed. Tears formed in her eyes and I took her arm.

Mrs. Smith stood at the door and waved as we left her yard. I stopped and handed Evie off to Andy.

"I'll meet you guys back at the cars." I bounded back to Mrs. Smith and held out my hand to take hers. "You're not alone, Mrs. Smith. Your husband is here, working on the house. He's happy and he's waiting for you whenever you're ready." I squeezed her hands. "You're not alone."

She looked up at me, her eyes full of surprise and something deeper, something like relief. A smile broke on her face and she squeezed my hands back. "Thank you, young lady. Thank you so much."

Back in the car, Evie ripped the envelope open and stared down at the check, her eyes wide. A tear slid out and ran down her cheek.

"Did your dad pay for any of the hospital bills?" she asked.

"A little. Your mom's work insurance paid for most of it."

"Well, I'll pay him back for whatever he paid and then, do you think your dad would take me to the bank and help me start a savings account…for college?" she asked. Then she smiled. "I can go to *college*, St. Louis!"

I smiled. "Yeah, for sure."

She placed the check back into the envelope reverently and tucked it safely into her coat pocket. She started the car and followed Andy and Tristan out of the parking spot. I waited until we were moving before I closed my eyes. We rode in silence and I could feel the road under the tires change from asphalt to gravel. I opened my eyes and slid down in my seat.

"Tired?" Evie asked.

"Not too bad."

We drove for several more miles and then slowed down as we got closer to the address. Andy's brake lights came on and then his blinker. He pulled into a small driveway covered by a tangle of brown and raspy weeds. They clung to our legs as we got out and stood at the end of the driveway. It led up to a fireplace standing in the middle of a field.

"Huh. Sarah Clifton," I said under my breath.

"Is she there?" Evie asked from my side.

I walked a little closer and stood in the middle of the place where a house once stood. I felt around for anyone and was tugged by something near the fireplace. I walked over and took off a glove, placing my hand on the cold, smooth stone.

A moment later, the house stood around me, little more than a cabin with a large room and a smaller bedroom off to the side. The floor was dirt and a fire blazed in the fireplace as a young woman leaned over to stir something in a pot. She wore a long dress and an apron, her hair pulled into a low bun.

"This isn't right," I mumbled. As I said the words, the house morphed around me, and now it was filled with furniture and a bathroom had been added next to the bedroom. A woman sat in a rocking chair, knitting a scarf as she listened to a large radio standing in the corner. The announcer came on and told the audience that the Grand Ole Opry would continue after these messages.

"It's the nineteen fifties," I said. "I think..." I looked closer. "She doesn't have a wedding ring. Sam said his daughter was married."

Andy's voice came through in waves. "Maybe she got a divorce."

I sighed. I didn't want to touch her, but it didn't seem like there was any other way. I reached out, but a moment before I touched her, Evie placed her hand on my arm.

"There has to be another way," she said as the previous house melted away and I was standing in the middle of a field again. "Don't you know anyone who would have been alive around the time Sarah was? Someone who might have known her?" Her eyes were unwavering.

I sighed and then nodded slowly. "My grandma."

CHAPTER 28

When we got to my house, dad was working in his office. He looked up as we walked through the living room.

"Marissa?" he said from the doorway. "Come talk to me for a minute?"

"We'll be in your room," Evie said.

I watched them leave and then went into Dad's office. I sat down in a chair and folded my arms over my chest.

"Still mad, huh?" He leaned back in his chair.

I blinked innocently. "Whatever would I be upset about? Gee, I can't think of anything that was said that was *completely* unfair."

He chuckled. "I get it. You have to understand that I'm worried about you, about Genevieve. I'm even worried about those other friends of yours."

"So, you're not bending on this?" I uncrossed my arms and stood up.

He shook his head. "I'm sorry, Peanut. When it comes to your safety, I have to put my foot down."

I narrowed my eyes. "Hypocrite," I said under my breath and turned to go.

"I'm not a hypocrite because I chose not to see the spirits anymore. I'd be a hypocrite if I let my teenage daughter mess with things that I know can be dangerous."

We stood, staring at one another across the expanse of his desk, neither willing to bend.

There was a small knock at the door and Evie came in. "I thought I could talk to your dad about this?" She held up the envelope that Mrs. Smith had given her.

"He's all yours," I said and turned to walk out.

"This isn't over," he said.

"It is for now," I said over my shoulder. Fuming, I stood in the dining room once I left his office.

"Psst."

I turned to see Evie standing at my dad's office door. She darted her eyes to the kitchen and raised her eyebrows, and then closed the glass doors behind her.

I sighed and walked into the kitchen. My grandma moved around the kitchen, making breakfast. I made my way over to the counter and stood, leaning against it. She looked so peaceful, happy even, as she made breakfast in her bright little kitchen. My grandpa sat behind his newspaper, his leg propped up.

I closed my eyes and took a deep breath. "This is for Sam," I said, reaching out toward my grandma's slightly stooped back.

"You know, you can just ask me."

My eyes whipped open and I almost fell on the floor.

My grandma stood before me, her blue eyes right on me as she held a wooden spoon in her hand.

"Y-you can see me?"

She smiled. "Of course. I can see you all."

"I-I don't understand."

"Don't stutter, and close your mouth. It's unbecoming for a young lady."

I snapped my mouth shut and stared at her. "Excuse me, but exactly *how* are you able to see me?"

She smiled and pointed at the kitchen chair with her spoon. "Sit down. I'll tell you all about it."

I walked on stiff legs over to the chair and sat down, watching as she moved away from the counter. She walked over to the chair and sat down across from me. Grandpa cleared his throat and she glanced over at him.

"I can't be long. He'll notice that I'm gone and go looking for me."

I shook my head. "Go looking for you?"

"Yes, as long as I stay here, making breakfast, he's happy. We're together and well, we're happy. If he notices that I'm gone, he starts to worry. It makes him so sad." She smiled at him and placed the spoon on the table. "Now, I'm sure you have a million questions, but you need to listen first."

"Yes, ma'am." My mind was spinning and I tried to take a deep breath and calm myself so I could catch everything she said. My heart raced and I could feel the energy draining from me, but at a much slower pace than ever before. I only had a moment to marvel at that before she started speaking.

"Like you and your father, I also have the ability to see spirits. I grew up in a time that didn't allow for fancies like that, though. My mother was frightened of it, and because of that, I was frightened of it. The country was coming out of the Great Depression and I had to help my parents make ends meet. My father was quite wealthy before the market crash, but afterwards, he and my mother barely scraped by. It wasn't until later in life, after I left and got married to your grandfather that they found a way to have a comfortable life together."

"So you could see ghosts?"

"Yes, but I didn't see any use for it, so I ignored it. I hoped that your father would grow up without the ability. No such luck, though." She sighed and smoothed her skirt with wrinkled hands.

"He said that you told him that the kids would make fun of him."

She looked up at me. "What else was I to do? People talk in a small town and I was afraid they would take him away from us. Put him in a home."

"He spent years of his life worried that he had disappointed you."

A strange look passed across her face. "It wasn't me that he disappointed. Your grandfather wouldn't have understood. I hid my own abilities from him and made sure your father did the same. Do you know what it's like to grow up…" she stopped, her eyes wide. Then, quieter, "I suppose that you do."

Grandpa turned the page of his paper and the noise filled the kitchen.

"You have to get back soon," I said. "I need to know if you knew a Sarah who lived in town during the early 1900s. She used to be a Johnson but we don't know her married name."

Grandma picked up her spoon and started back to the counter.

"I need to know! There's a ghost in trouble!"

She turned around. Her eyes were worried and she looked around the kitchen uncomfortably. "Now, you listen here. You are playing with things in this town that no young girl should be messing with. Leave well enough alone and stop looking for trouble. Because, believe you me, you can find plenty of it in this town."

I stood up. "I have to know. We've tried to find her because we want to help Sam. He's taking spirits to the darkness."

Recognition and then fear passed into her eyes. "Then, it's started."

"What? What's started?"

"Quiet down, now." She walked over and took hold of my arm. Energy snapped through me and everything came into crystalline focus. I felt completely recharged and stronger than I'd ever felt. "You come from a long line of seers. Your father, my mother, my grandfather, and me. Your grandmother's name was Elizabeth *Sarah* Miller. Before she was married, she was a Johnson." She stood back, regarding me with bright, watchful eyes.

"Sam is, is my *great-great-grandfather?*" I stood there, reeling from what she told me.

My grandfather put his paper down and looked around the kitchen. "Lydia? Dear, where are you?"

"I have to go," she said. "She's at 1113 Sycamore." Then, she faded a bit and slipped back into the memory. "I'm right here, dear." She walked over and gave my grandpa a kiss on the cheek. I hadn't seen this in the loop before, but then, she started making biscuits again, rolling the dough into a long roll. My grandfather nodded and started reading his paper again.

I took a deep breath and headed up the stairs. When I got to my room, I opened the door and closed it, resting my back against its surface.

Andy and Tristan were watching TV and looked up when I came in. They both stood up.

"What's wrong?"

"Anderson?"

I shook my head and walked over to my bed, sitting down and staring at the floor. "He's my great-great-grandfather."

"Who?" Tristan knelt on the floor in front of me. "Who's your great-great-grandfather?"

I sat there, not sure what I was going to do with this new information.

The door opened and closed. Evie walked in. "What's going on?"

Tristan turned. "She said that he's her great-great-grandfather."

She flopped down on the futon. "Who?"

I turned to look at her. "Sam."

Chapter 29

"He's your great-great-grandfather?"

"Your grandma was able to see and talk to you this whole time?"

"Your whole *family* can see ghosts?"

The questions flew around me, not quite reaching me as I sat on the bed, rolling what I'd found out around in my head. My phone buzzed and I pulled it out, staring at the screen.

Evie gently took the phone from me. She read the message. "It's Grant. Do you want him to come here?"

I took a deep breath. "Why not? Apparently, I come from a long line of freaks. What's not to love about that?"

She cocked her head to the side. "I'm going to text him and let him know he can meet us here." Her fingers flew over the screen. "And, you're not a freak." She gave me a sideways glance.

"Marissa," Tristan said, "we need to go to Sarah's house. We need to help Sam."

"My dad will never let me go."

Evie looked at me. "What if he doesn't know?"

I stared at her. "You mean, sneaking out?"

"That's exactly what I mean. He's working on a big case, so he'll be at that for the rest of the afternoon."

I swallowed. *Sneaking out?*

"We'll be gone an hour, maybe two tops."

"What if he comes up here and we're gone?"

"I'll leave a note on the fridge. We'll tell him that Grant came by and picked us up and we went for burgers in Eagleton. We didn't want to bother him, but he should text us if he wants us to bring him some carry-out."

I shook my head. "I don't like it. I've never snuck out before."

She got up and walked over to the door. Her hand on the doorknob, she turned to look at me. "Well, head on downstairs and ask him if he's okay with us totally going against what he told you last night. Ask him if it's okay to go out, build a portal, and help a ghost out of the darkness. I'm *sure* he'll be fine with it."

"Shut up," I snarled. My stomach twisted uncomfortably and then I felt nausea set in. "If he catches me, I'll be grounded forever."

"This is bigger than getting grounded for a few days," Evie said quietly. "This is Sam's soul."

I sat up. "But, now, it's family. Maybe he'd be willing to let us go if he knows it's family."

"Marissa," Evie said, "your grandma's been able to talk to you and your dad the whole time and she chose not to. How do you think he'll feel about that?"

Guilt pressed down on me. "He'd feel terrible." I blinked. "Fine."

Evie texted Grant to let him know to meet us at the end of the driveway and then she scrawled a note on a piece of paper. We opened the door and snuck down the back staircase. I reached the bottom and peeked around the wall. I could see the office doors and they were closed. I motioned for the group to head into the kitchen and then I followed. Andy and Tristan were at the backdoor by the time I made it into the kitchen. Evie stood next to the basement door, her coat in one hand and mine in the other. She had tacked the note to the refrigerator.

The backdoor squeaked as we opened it and I held my breath, listening for my dad. When it stayed quiet, we stepped out onto the porch and pulled the door closed behind us. I thought maybe I'd feel better the further away from the house we got.

I didn't.

My stomach churned as we wound our way behind the barn and walked up the driveway along the wooded area to hide our tracks. A storm was building in the winter sky and the afternoon had grown gloomy and drab under a bruised gray sky. I kept looking over my shoulder, sure that I would see the front door to the house open and my dad's silhouette shouting at us to come back. Nothing happened, though, and by the time we reached the end of the driveway, I was almost frozen solid. Grant's car slid out of the gloom and we piled in.

"Hey," he said, leaning over to kiss my cheek. "You're cold."

"1113 Sycamore," Tristan said. "It's been renamed to a county road, but I can get us there. Go straight and then turn off on Highway O."

Grant stepped on the gas and the powerful engine roared and we headed off down the road. The ride was quiet for a few minutes, then Grant broke the silence. "So, is anyone going to tell me why I have a car full of fugitives?"

I let the group fill him in while I stared out the window at the darkening trees sliding by. Something was unsettling me and I couldn't put my finger on it. I closed my eyes and rested my forehead against the cool window. Grant's hand was warm on my leg and I let myself slip, telling myself that it was okay, I would need my strength later.

When the car finally stopped, I blinked, trying to orient myself in the country. I got out of the car and felt a pull toward the field to our side. I managed to climb my way up the embankment and stood looking out over the field of snow. The clouds rolled above, lowering with the promise of snow. It made me feel claustrophobic.

Looking back at the road, I recognized the area. "This is close to Amalie's," I said as Evie came up the hill to stand beside me. "Remember? You saw a disturbance here when we were looking for the little girl's house?"

Evie nodded. "I remember. But I don't see anything now."

"Can you still see them? The disturbances? At all?"

"Come on," she said and set out across the field. We followed. The going was tough. The corn had been cut earlier that fall, but about six inches of corn stalk was left and would be turned under in the spring. We tripped our way to a small grove of trees in the distance.

As we came up to the first line of trees, Evie let out a small gasp. I looked up from my feet and sucked in a breath. *I drew this.*

There in the grove was a small, two-story Victorian. Long, straggly weeds covered the front yard, rising out of the dusting of snow that had been allowed through the branches of the trees. The main part of the house was rectangular and there were two windows at the top of the second floor and two on the front of the house, flanking a front door covered by a triangular porch with a small deck on the upper floor, surrounded on three sides by an intricate railing. The fourth side had succumbed to the rot and fallen away, hanging at an odd angle from the eaves.

"I guess we found it," Andy said as he whipped out a camera and started recording.

"Do you bring that thing everywhere?" Grant asked.

Andy waggled his eyebrows at Grant and then started narrating as he walked up to the house, swinging the camera around to take in all of the old building. He turned to look at me. "Do your stuff, Anderson."

I closed my eyes, concentrating on the feeling of the house, the whispers of its past. I heard a songbird and opened my eyes. It was a beautiful spring day and the house was surrounded by wildflowers. They offset the fresh whitewash on its slat boards and the windows gleamed in the sunlight that wandered down from the trees. A gentle breeze tossed the baby green leaves and I could smell spring in the air. I smiled.

"There she goes," Andy said.

I walked toward the house, prodded gently by the breeze behind me. As I walked, I caught the sound of singing on the wind. It was a beautiful song, somehow familiar, but not one I knew. I followed it up to the front door.

"Keep an eye on her," Tristan said to Grant. "She can't see this time, only the way it looked when Sarah lived here."

The living room was filled with opulent furniture. An ornate mirror hung above the mantle and a plush rug spread out over the hardwood floors. I felt someone's hands on my shoulders, directing me along the side of the living room.

"The floor is gone here," Grant said in my ear.

I smiled again. "Thanks." He let go as I passed the staircase. I stopped then and cocked my head, listening. "Upstairs," I said. I started up the stairs and felt hands guiding me again. I was helped to skip a couple of steps near the top and then I stood in the upstairs hallway.

The rooms to either side of me were ornate and filled with expensive furniture like the living room below. I followed the hallway to the second room on the right. In the room was a massive canopy bed with a heavy dresser and two velvet-covered chairs in the corner by the window. The double doors opened up to the porch over the front door. On the deck were a pair of matching Adirondack chairs. In one, a woman sat, humming a tune.

"Sarah," I said as I went through the door and stood on the porch. I looked down at her. Her features were beautiful and she had green eyes and long brown hair, just like me. "My great-grandma," I whispered. "Hi."

She smiled, reading a book and humming. Her features were calm and she was happy. I could feel contentment rolling off her and I couldn't help smiling. As I stood there, visions of her happy memories scrolled through my head. Her running through the creek as a small girl, her having my grandmother, she and her husband dancing, and finally, the day she got married. She was a beautiful bride and so full of excitement for this new life she was about to embark upon.

I closed my eyes and opened them again. The house was decrepit and it was cold again.

Grant stood next to me, almost in a crouching position.

"Whatcha' doin?" I asked.

He stood up straight. "I didn't want you to get hurt. Can you see the *now* now?"

I took a shaky breath. "Yeah."

Evie and Tristan stood below in the yard looking up at us, a circle of grass tamped down with sticks around it.

"She's happy!" I shouted down. "We need Sam to see this!"

"We're ready down here," Evie said. "We just need Sarah."

"Okay," I said. I closed my eyes and felt for Sarah's spirit. I could hear Evie down below, chanting the same thing the girl in the video had chanted. I opened my eyes when I felt the atmosphere change and Sarah sat before me again. She turned a page in her book and I reached out to touch her.

The moment my fingertip made contact with her shoulder, a huge boom rushed at me. I was ready for it and braced myself against the onslaught of electricity that I felt. A moment later, Sarah stood before me in her wedding dress, her eyes questioning but calm.

"Hi, Sarah," I said. "My name is Marissa and I'm your great-granddaughter."

She smiled, her eyes kind and soft. "Then, that means that I am dead and someone is in danger."

CHAPTER 30

I stood gaping at Sarah for a moment. "Y-you know about Sam?"

Her kind eyes softened. "My father."

"He's in trouble. He saved a friend of mine and he was taken by a dark spirit. We think that the darkness is twisting his memories, making him see things that didn't happen." I looked up at her. She remained calm, her countenance pleasant and bathed in a lightness. "Um, my friend, Evie told us that's what happened to her when she was down there. We thought maybe it was happening to him, too."

She smiled and peered over the railing of the porch. She looked down at Evie and Tristan and bowed her head, closing her eyes in a delicate gesture. Then, she turned to look at me. "And you thought his happiest memory might be of me?"

I shrugged. "Maybe?"

She held the skirt of her wedding dress wide. "This should tell you that you are right."

I furrowed my brow. "I don't understand."

"The only time I saw my father after he died was the day I got married. My new husband and I went into the courthouse to file the license, and on our way out, I turned and looked at the porch of the building." Her face took on a wistful quality as she spoke. "I saw him. He stood there, staring out at me. I could feel the love pouring out of his spirit toward me."

"Did you try to talk to him?" I swallowed. "I mean, did you have the same powers I have?"

She smiled sadly. "I was forced to hide my powers. From a young age, I learned that having the ability to see spirits was one that was feared. My grandmother," her voice caught a hard edge, "forbade me from *seeing* things. I hid it from my family and then I hid it from my husband."

I glanced over at Grant. "Wouldn't your husband have believed you?"

She smiled again. "Perhaps, but I was unwilling to give him the chance to believe it or not. He was my husband. We were very wealthy and very happy. We welcomed our only child, Lydia, into our world during my thirty-second year and then, shortly after her birth, the Great Depression came. There was no time for frivolity. We lost almost everything during those years. They were hard times." A cloud passed over her face. Her eyes darted over to Grant. "But this one, he knows about your ability?"

I followed her gaze. Grant cocked his head to the side. "Yeah," I said, "he knows."

"What is your intention?" she asked.

"Well, I mean, we've only been dating for a few weeks and he's at school all the way in Kansas City..." I trailed off as Sarah began to laugh.

She hid her mouth behind her hand in a dainty gesture.

"What's going on?" Grant asked.

"Well, she's laughing at me."

"Oh, I apologize. I am not laughing at you. I only meant, what are your intentions to help my father?"

Mental head smack. "Right, um, so Evie and Tristan have built a portal. We thought if Sam could see you and see that you're fine, he would be able to escape from the darkness."

She stared at me. "And this will work?"

"Do you have a better idea?" I asked. Then, to soften the tone, "It's the only way we know to save him."

"Then, we should not waste any more time. The hour grows late." Sarah stepped forward and placed a gentle hand on my cheek. Electricity passed between us. "You are so pretty. I wish I could have known you."

I smiled and reached up to touch her hand. "Me, too."

"Come, let's go."

I followed her as she passed through the bedroom, past the boys, and through the door beyond. Grant reached out to touch my arm.

"Can you see?" he asked.

"Yeah, she's here in our time now."

"Are you going to fill us in on that conversation, Anderson?"

"Yeah, later, come on. We're going to try to get Sam in the portal."

When we reached the front yard, the sun had completely set and evening crept through the trees, snaking along the ground and bringing with it an icy chill. I wrapped my coat around me and was thankful when I felt the warm pressure of Grant's arm as he draped it over my shoulders.

Sarah walked to the edge of the circle and stood quietly. She turned to look at me. "What now?"

I walked over.

"Um, we saw a girl open a portal, but we're not sure we're doing it right," Evie said.

"Nothing's happening," Tristan reported.

We stood in silence, the wind whipping our hair.

"Aren't the ghosts supposed to build the portal?" Grant asked.

We all turned to look at him.

He took a step back, his arm falling from my shoulders. "I only meant that it seems like any other time Sam has come through, the ghosts have been the ones building it."

I closed my eyes and shook my head. "I never thought of that." Then, I looked at Sarah. "Can you build a circle?"

"With what?"

I searched the group with my eyes. "Any ideas?"

"If she tries to build it with sticks, it could take a while." Tristan was on his phone, swiping through screens.

"I don't think you'll find an answer to this on that," I mumbled.

He shot me a glare and continued to scroll, his face lit up in the blue light from the screen.

"What if we build most of the circle and she puts in the last piece?" Evie offered.

"It can't hurt to try. Sarah, do you think you could put in the last stick to complete the circle?"

She furrowed her brow, the action delicate. "I can certainly try."

"Here," I said, stooping over to grab a stick from the edge of the circle, "take this and place it back right here." I indicated the place with my other hand.

Sarah pressed her lips together in a familiar motion and I realized I was pressing my lips together in concentration, too. Reaching out, her hand hovered above the stick in mine. She reached down and attempted to grab the stick. Her hand went right through it. She tried several times with the same result.

Frustrated, I said, "She's trying, but she can't get hold of it. What now?"

"Maybe it has to be an object that was here when she was," Evie said, her eyes darting around the yard.

"Hold on!" Andy put his camera down on the ground and ran up into the house. He came out a moment later, holding a piece of floorboard above his head triumphantly. "Try this! But let me get my camera first!" He handed the splintered piece of wood to me and then picked up his camera and started shooting again. "Okay, go!"

I held the piece of wood in my hand, trying to keep it steady even though I was shivering like crazy at this point. My teeth chattered and I bit down on them to stop the sound.

Sarah reached down and on the second try she was able to wrap her fingers around the wood, pulling it out of my hands and holding it in the air.

"Wicked," Andy mumbled.

I imagined that the whole group was as excited as he was to see a piece of wood floating in the air. I had a fleeting sense of nostalgia for the first weeks we went together to the cemetery, looking for proof of paranormal activity. Now, things were so complicated. I shook my head, clearing it as Sarah moved the wood into the circle, completing it on the ground.

We all stood silently, watching and listening for any movement or sound.

Nothing happened.

"Nothing's happening," Evie said.

"Great. What now?"

"I think we're back to Sarah building the whole circle."

I sighed. "That will take too long."

"Wait," Sarah said. She reached up and unpinned her long veil from her headpiece. It fluttered on the breeze, hanging in a cloud around her. "I can make this into a circle. Will that work?"

"Brilliant! Here," I kicked the sticks out of the smooth cleared area.

"That only took us thirty minutes to build," Evie muttered.

"She's going to use her veil."

"Oh."

Sarah knelt down on the ground in front of the small clearing, her white dress billowing out and falling in a circle of light around her. Her eyes were focused on her task as she spread the veil into a circle.

"Is she doing it?" Andy asked.

I nodded. The circle closed and I felt the air around me crackle. "I think it's working. Sarah, do you see anything?"

She shook her head once and then leaned forward, peering into the circle. "Wait but a moment, I think, no!" Her hand flew up to her mouth and I ran to her side, kneeling down beside her, my feet tracking snow onto her skirt.

There, in the circle, was a shimmering surface, like a lake that had been disturbed by a breeze. Through the shimmering, I could make out another level. Below the surface, was the cavern underneath the basement of the courthouse. In the cavern was a darkness that enveloped everything around it. A huge wind started through the trees and some branches rained down on us.

"What's happening?" Evie shouted above the din.

I cleared my throat. "I can see it. I can see the darkness."

A moment later, a sound like a truck driving through the woods reached my ears. I looked up, half expecting to see headlights bearing down on us in the darkness of the gathering evening. The shimmering in the circle of the veil grew darker, more sinister, and, as both Sarah and I backed away from it, a dark light shot up through its center, obliterating every happy feeling I'd ever had. I could feel my mother slipping away, saying goodbye to Piper, and my dad looking at me with disappointment as I left his office earlier that day. I reached over and pulled Sarah back from the column of darkness as it rose into the sky from the portal. Her face was pulled tight in a silent scream and I could feel the sadness rolling off her.

A moment later, the darkness disappeared, sending out shards of dark emotions in every direction.

Evie cried out and Tristan dropped his phone. Andy's hands gripped the camera, his knuckles turning white. I looked at Grant and he stared back at me, his gaze cold and distant. He shook his head slowly in disgust as he glared at me. My heart twisted painfully in my chest and I opened my mouth to say something to him. I couldn't eek a sound out of the bottomless pit of despair that I felt coming off me in waves.

Then, the feeling ebbed for a moment and a figure stepped from the circle.

It was Sam.

CHAPTER 31

Sam stood, staring around at our faces, his movements almost serpentine as his eyes peered out from under the hoods of his brow. He swept his gaze to me. The dark circles under his eyes made them more powerful somehow, and it felt like he was looking into my soul. His lips parted in a sneer. "Marisssssa..." He took a step toward me, his hands reaching out.

I heard movement before I saw it, and suddenly, Evie was in front of me, quickly followed by Tristan, Andy, and Grant.

"You're going to have to go through us to get to her," Tristan said.

With a barrier of bodies between us, my mind cleared a bit and I was able to form a thought. "You, you can see him?"

Andy nodded his head without looking back. He was still filming.

Sam smiled, his eyes glittering and hollow. "It wants her." His voice was barely a hiss, but it filled up the space around us, bounced off the treetops, and ratcheted back down to our ears. He walked forward again and Evie threw her hands up, aiming to bar him as she had before.

Sam took one look at her and swatted her away like a mosquito. She went flying in the air, landing with a grunt a few feet away.

"Evie!"

"I'm okay," she said as she tried to sit up.

Sam advanced, his head tilted down, staring at me through eyes filled with hate. He brought his hands into an X in front of his chest and then swept them down and out. The air flexed, and Tristan and Andy flew in opposite directions. Only Grant stood between the advancing monster and me.

"Stop!" Grant said, his voice deep and resonating as it rose into the air. "She's your great-great-granddaughter!"

Sam's eyebrow rose slightly, creating a triangle above his dark eye. A smile twisted the corner of his mouth. "Yes, she is." With that, he made a slashing motion at Grant.

Grant cried out and doubled over, holding his stomach.

Fury ran hot through my body and I stepped around Grant. "Leave him alone!" Spittle flew from my mouth as I screamed at Sam.

Grant held out his arm, placing it in front of me and attempting to push me back behind him. Tristan and Andy were on their feet and advancing on Sam. Evie had also found her feet and she was circling behind him, her eyes intent on his back.

I caught her gaze and shook my head slightly. *It's too dangerous.*

"Father?"

Sarah's gentle voice came from somewhere behind me, and as the word left her lips, time froze. Evie stopped mid-crouch and Andy and Tristan looked like mannequins caught mid-stride. Grant glared up at Sam, his arm still in front of me, protecting me as best he could.

Sam's attention left me and he swung around to look at Sarah.

She stood near the front porch, her wedding dress reflecting the light of the rising moon, creating a halo of light around her. "Father, it's me."

Sam's eyes glinted in the moonlight reflecting off her dress. He leaned forward, peering at her as though he were looking through a thick fog. He cried out, the sound of anguish passing through his lips and resonating in my soul as he stared at her. He whipped his head back and forth, the cry dying on his lips.

"Father, it's your little Sarah. Look at me." She took a step forward, her skirt rustling in the cold air. She held a bouquet of flowers in her hands and I caught the scent of roses as she neared. "Father?"

I looked at my friends, frozen in time. My heart ached. I hadn't meant to bring them into danger.

Sam moved toward Sarah, his movements jerky, as if he was fighting against an internal demon. As he walked, his eyes lightened and came forward on his face. And then he was there. He was Sam.

"Sarah?" His voice was plaintive, desperate. "Sarah, is that you?"

Her eyes filled with tears and she let out a laugh like a bark. "Yes, it's me. Look, I'm here. I'm okay."

He furrowed his brow, tears forming in his eyes. "Sarah?" His voice held disbelief.

I took the opportunity. "Sam, you went into the darkness to save Evie. We think it took your memories and twisted them."

He turned to look at me, his face waffling between desperation and evil. He was fighting hard, but as I looked into his eyes, I knew he was losing the fight.

I spoke quickly. "Sam, you have to get out of there. You have to remember Sarah as she is. She's fine. We're all fine."

Recognition filled his eyes and he saw me, really saw me. "Marissa."

"Yes, Sam, you have to stop this. You have to get out."

He shook his head, blind fear taking over his features. He glanced behind him at the circle on the ground. When he turned back, his eyes were filled with horror. "I'm so sorry, Marissa, for what I've done. I thought, I thought it was the only way to…" He turned sad eyes to Sarah. "You were on fire." His voice caught in his throat. "You were burning. My sweet Sarah."

A sound like a freight train came from the circle and a massive column of black smoke rose from the clearing, winding out and grabbing hold of Sam with insistent threads.

"No!" I shouted.

The spell was broken and everyone began to move again. Sam's eyes went dark and vacant again and he lunged.

Sarah stepped in front of me at the last moment, crying out as Sam's arms circled her, his clawed fingers digging into the tender flesh at the tops of her arms. He enveloped her and dragged her toward the circle a few feet away. She turned to look at me, her gentle eyes suddenly overcome by blackness.

"Sarah!" I shouted. I threw myself forward, my arms reaching out toward her. Evie was beside me, holding onto me, pulling me back. Then, they were all there, holding onto me. My forward momentum broke as the smoke holding Sam and Sarah rose up and then plunged down through the circle of the veil, sending an explosion out across the yard. I tumbled back on my friends and we landed in a pile on the ground as the burning embers of the veil floated in the air around us.

"No, he took Sarah!" I scrambled up and across the ground, my hands burning on the remnants of her veil as they fell around me. At the circle, I swept my hands across the dirt, and then scratched at the ground with my fingernails.

"St. Louis?" Evie's voice was quiet and I could feel her kneel down beside me. "They're gone."

"No," I cried, my nose running. I swiped at it with the sleeve of my coat. "No, Evie, they can't be gone. It wasn't supposed to be like this!"

"Shhh," she said, smoothing my hair from my face.

I looked up at her and the dam broke open, my tears flowing down my face. I leaned into her, allowing her coat to soak up a few of my sobs. Then, I wiped my eyes angrily and stood up, my jaw set and my teeth gritting together painfully.

I watched Tristan and Andy as they supported Grant between them. "I am so sorry," I said, anger welling up in my stomach. Sam was a monster and he had hurt my friends and taken my great-grandmother.

"He's still in there," Evie said quietly. "I know you could see it, too."

"Whatever has hold of him isn't going to give him up easily," Tristan said.

"Y-you guys could see him?" I asked.

"Yeah, he's really strong, Anderson."

I pressed my lips together. "He has to be stopped."

"But, um, not tonight," Tristan said. He nodded his head in Grant's direction.

"Oh my God. Are you okay?" I ran over to his side.

He looked up at me with a crooked grin. "Nothing some peroxide won't cure." He lifted his coat and I saw four angry red welts rising amid the muscles on his stomach.

"Let's go home," Evie said.

I followed numbly.

As Grant drove through the night, he glanced over at me. "What's the plan now?"

"You mean, besides moving out of this stupid town?"

"You don't mean that."

I shook my head. "I don't understand. He was right there. We got through to him."

"He said he was sorry," Andy said. "I'm watching the recording now. He said he was sorry for what he'd done. What do you think he meant?"

I shook my head. It felt like it was filled with cotton. Closing my eyes, I rolled my head from side to side, the bones in my neck popping. It didn't release any of the tension though, and I gritted my teeth against the terrible feeling rising in my middle.

Grant reached over and placed a warm hand on my leg. "Let's get you home, okay?"

I smiled, my eyelids fighting to close.

"Yeah, I think home would be good."

CHAPTER 32

I woke up when the car stopped.

Grant parked to the side of the road at the end of the driveway. "You want me to come in with you?"

I shook my head, trying inauspiciously to wipe the drool from the side of my mouth. *Sexy, Marissa.* "It's okay. I'm not sure what my dad's going to do with us sneaking out and everything."

"He didn't text, so maybe you're in the clear."

"Maybe." I got out of the car and pulled the zipper up on my coat.

Tristan, Andy, and Evie walked up the driveway a bit, giving Grant and me a chance to say goodbye.

Grant stood in front of me, his eyes soft as he gazed down at me. He reached up to move a tendril of hair from my forehead. "What's wrong?" He smiled.

"Don't you think this is all a bit, too much? I mean, really, Grant, I'm the last in a long line of ghost-seers, and my great-great-grandpa is out to kill me from the grave. You didn't sign up for this."

"Who says I didn't? Girls with psychotic dead great-great-grandpas are kinda' my thing." He swept his hair out of his eyes and they sparkled down at me. "Seriously. I'm not going anywhere." He wrapped me in a huge hug and kissed the top of my head.

"You looked at me tonight like you hated me," I said, my voice muffled by his coat.

He held me at arm's length. "I did?"

"Yeah, when Sam came out, I looked over at you and you were staring at me with complete disgust. Like you hated me."

His eyes softened. "I could never hate you," he said, leaning down to kiss my cheek.

"Still." I let the word hang between us.

He tilted his head to the side. "When Sam came out, I felt it, too. I looked at you, and you were gone. Not like poof, gone, but your eyes were completely vacant. You were standing there, in front of me, but you weren't *there* anymore." He furrowed his brow. "It scared me." He pulled me to him again.

Andy cleared his throat. "Can't feel my toes, Anderson."

I smiled. "See you soon?"

"I'll be back home before you know it." Grant tilted my chin up and kissed my lips. "I love you," he murmured.

"I love you, too," I whispered.

I caught up with the others as Grant drove away to head back to school. We made our way up the driveway along the side again, our feet sinking into the thick blanket of snow.

"The light's still on in the office," I noted as we walked. "Do you think we got away with it?" The question died in my throat as we approached the house. "Why is the front door open?" I broke into a run and pounded up the front porch steps. I stepped into the house and wiggled out of my coat, dropping it on the floor of the living room as I rounded the corner. Dad's office was empty. An oily sick feeling coated my insides.

"Dad?"

Evie closed the door behind Andy and Tristan. "He's probably on the phone with military school," she said.

I ignored her. "Andy, check upstairs?"

"On it," he quipped, heading up the stairs like a secret agent. He slid along the wall and then darted around the corner at the landing.

"Good grief." Tristan rolled his eyes. "I'm sure he's fine, Marissa." He placed a comforting hand on my shoulder.

I shrugged it off and headed through the living room to the dining room. "Dad?"

Andy met us at the bottom of the stairs at the entrance to the kitchen. He shook his head. "He's not up there."

I stepped into the kitchen.

Several things hit me at once.

Something about the kitchen felt wrong, off-kilter somehow. I looked at the table and saw my grandfather. The newspaper had fallen to the ground and he sat looking around the kitchen.

"Marissa's in trouble. Come quick. Marissa's in trouble. Come quick. Marissa's in trouble. Come quick..." Tears rolled down his cheeks and a black mist roiled around his feet.

I whirled around to look at the counter and my hand flew up to my mouth. My grandmother was gone. There was a circle of dough on a bed of flour on the counter.

I turned wide eyes to Evie. "Where is she?"

"Your grandmother?"

"Yes! She made a portal from the dough she was making."

"Marissa's in trouble. Come quick. Marissa's in trouble. Come quick…"

"Did Sam get to her?" Andy stood in the middle of the kitchen, his breath hanging in a cloud in front of his face.

That's wrong. Why is it cold in here?

I shook my head. "I don't think so. She kissed my grandpa goodbye while I was standing there."

"Well, if she's related to you, she probably went to help Sam herself," Evie said. She shivered.

That's wrong, too.

I swung my gaze from the countertop to the refrigerator. "Your note's gone."

Maybe we forgot to leave one. I shook my head, trying to shake the awful feeling. I felt like I was trying to think through mud and my brain wasn't making connections fast enough.

I shivered. *Why is it so cold in here?*

Then, I turned my head.

The back door stood wide open, the winter wind sending ice particles skittering across the linoleum. I took a step toward the open door, my legs stiff. "Dad?" A million worst case scenarios ran through my head as I stepped out on the back porch.

Grandpa's frail voice followed me. "Marissa's in trouble. Come quick. Marissa's in trouble. Come quick..."

I opened the screen door and stepped down. The group followed me, clustered around me in the darkness.

I cried out. There, in the deep snow, were my dad's footprints. They were spaced wide apart as if he had been running.

"Marissa's in trouble. Come quick. Marissa's in trouble. Come quick..."

Running into the woods behind the house.

"Marissa's in trouble. Come quick. Marissa's in trouble. Come quick..."

Toward the cave.

"Marissa's in trouble. Come quick. Marissa's in trouble. Come quick..."

"Dad!" I screamed into the night.

Acknowledgements

Thank you, first, to my husband and daughter who are the greatest sources of support and love a writer could ask for.

Thank you to Amanda Booloodian for all of the encouragement and support. Thank you to my wonderful beta readers, Roger Bolle and Julie Bolle, who never cease to amaze me with their thoughts and input.

Thank you to my faithful editor, Frankie Sutton, for her feedback and attention to detail. Thank you, as well, to Covered Creatively for another beautiful cover design and to Vicki Deiter for her formatting expertise.

Ghost Hunters Society Series:

Book One: The Weeping Bridge
Book Two: The Devil Doll
Book Three: The Burning Bride
Book Four: The Widow's Locket
Book Five: The Hoodoo Princess

Other YA books by Adria Waters:

Always Sweet Sixteen
The Edge of Lucidity

About The Author

Adria Waters is the author of the Ghost Hunters Society series and has seen ghosts all her life. She loves exploring the paranormal and goes on ghost tours in every place she visits. When she's not hunting ghosts, she loves torturing her family with road trips across the country to see every single sightseeing opportunity in the United States. Adria lives in Missouri with her very patient husband, her not-so-patient daughter, a herd of cats who insist that they are human, and various little spirits that pop up to say "hello" once in a while.

You can find out more about Adria and her writing at
www.AdriaWaters.com

www.ingramcontent.com/pod-product-compliance
Lightning Source LLC
Chambersburg PA
CBHW060355260626
47160CB00006B/2316